A
Harlequin
Romance

A LESSON IN LOVING

by

MARGARET WAY

Harlequin Books

TORONTO • LONDON • NEW YORK • AMSTERDAM • SYDNEY • WINNIPEG

Original hardcover edition published in 1975
by Mills & Boon Limited

SBN 373-01974-2

Harlequin edition published May, 1976

CHAPTER ONE

THERE were a great many things she had to do for herself, yet Rosslyn hesitated to leave. She was waiting for the parent, or parents, of her problem child, Kylie. It was already past four o'clock. Of course she had herself to blame. She had scheduled the meeting for some nebulous time 'after school', but all the classes, except Music, ended at three-thirty. Another fifteen minutes should do it, then she would be satisfied she had not failed in her duty. She felt in a strange kind of mood, the tenseness of anticipation giving way to a vague upset. The very children who most needed a close parent–teacher liaison were the ones who missed out on one. Like Kylie.

Kylie was a little monkey, as delightful to look upon as a Kate Greenaway illustration, and she was the talk of the school. There was no merit at all in behaving with Kylie. She had a fabulous capacity for disrupting herself and the rest of the class. What seemed to the other children as the perfectly normal thing to do made Kylie explode. Kylie was a disturbed child, forever in search of the sweet honey of attention, but Rosslyn was certain behind that turbulent, over-confident façade was a small girl who had to be treated with care.

Rosslyn's eyes were the key to her face, very large and liquid, almond-shaped and as gentle and sensitive as the fawn's they resembled. Rosslyn had a gift for handling children and constructively and imaginatively directing their energies, but she had a tendency towards taking to heart all their minor maladies and heartbreaks. For Kylie she had a special feeling of empathy, but she knew her view of the child was not shared by the rest of the staff, with whom Rossyln herself was intensely popular. Miss Keating, the headmistress, was of the opinion that Rosslyn was over-scrupulous about according to each of her small charges their own breathing space, and even Emma George of Arts and Crafts, a most dedicated lady, had flatly refused to have Rosslyn's protegée in her class at all. Decorating the walls of the Activities Centre, however appealingly, couldn't be considered at all. Kylie and Miss George were at war, but it was no secret that in the six months since Rosslyn had taken over the Fourth Form, Kylie had come closest to behaving like a reasonably well integrated student.

Now she had blackened her newly found respectability somewhat by restyling Amanda Weldon's Godiva-length locks, mercifully with Amanda's sworn approval but Mrs. Weldon's black outrage. Even when Kylie had been called into Miss Keating's intimidating presence, she had silenced both women by pointing out in her precocious, precise tones that the deed was a decided improvement and it opened out for 'Manda a whole new personality. The amazing thing was, it did, and this and not Kylie's spectacular action, nor the great excitement it engendered, saved her. That, and possibly the fact that her name was Ballinger.

Morlands had a very great respect for names and

fame and an accompanying unassailable bank balance, necessary to pay such exorbitant fees. It was very good for prestige to have a Ballinger at the school. Morlands took that kind of thing very seriously and it was a very good school in spite of it. Quicksilver Kylie, a thorn in everyone's side, had already at eight, with her fiery expressiveness and woefully misdirected capacity for leadership, the unmistakable aura of class, or belonging to a family of considerable attainment.

The Ballingers were among the landed élite of the State, one of the big pioneering families, a consistently superlative line of thoroughbreds, supplying as they did from the earliest days of settlement the statesmen, the cattle barons, the real estate tycoons, the financiers, the mining magnates, and now, astonishingly, as if to show there was not a field that was not open to them, an artist of the first rank: Derek Ballinger, Kylie's father. Rosslyn gave up her own decorative doodling and walked to the window, looking out over the golden-blue luminosity of late afternoon. From the long line of practice rooms came the agonized screech of a violin solo. A difficult instrument, the violin, she thought, wincing, but the orchestra did so need players. She only hoped the lesson would be over by the time the Ballingers arrived. An artist of quality himself, Derek Ballinger might take fright, and Rosslyn for one wouldn't have blamed him. It took severe self-discipline to remain at the window herself. Perhaps he would be accompanied by his trendy, much photographed wife? It was Kylie who painted the stunningly bleak picture of familial life. With every material benefit possible

7

offered to her, she seemed to crave the real warmth and shelter of a close parental commitment. Very likely the Ballingers loved their child. Kylie was clever despite herself and enchantingly pretty, but basically her febrile efforts to gain attention seemed to stem from the very lack of it at home.

Rosslyn was locked into this critical dissection, for she and Kylie, even on the days the sparks flew, could communicate. Kylie had a way of looking up suddenly and smiling in a way that made all the real Kylie shine through. Kylie had charm, for all her desperate naughtiness and her outrageous highly obstructive behaviour. At least the rate of incident had been put into her. On the other hand, in Rosslyn's class alone did Kylie *not* take unholy control. This meeting then was absolutely imperative before Kylie made her own position at the school untenable. Mrs. Weldon was an influential member of the school Board and the Ballingers had never been sighted. Kylie was brought to and taken home from school by some trusted member of the Ballinger staff.

The pity of it all was, Kylie had enormous potential. Improving her environment seemed to be her first love, and even her efforts in the Activities Room were as much a definite creative impulse as a deliberate piece of mayhem. Rosslyn, on seeing the Magic Rainbow, effect had been much entertained. It was just such an effect Kylie had been trying to get across, but Rosslyn alone on the staff grasped sight of this fact. Kylie, so absolutely vulnerable, or so she seemed to the admittedly tender-hearted Rosslyn. Her hands rested lightly on the windowsill and the sun touched her creamy gold skin. She was beginning to be a little angry with the Ballingers. Bad manners were unforgivable.

Outside the parrots and lorikeets were homing in to the blossom-laden trees. The grounds were beautiful, humming drowsily in the dusky blue sunlight. Even the unhappy violin solo was no longer in evidence. Rosslyn glanced down at her wrist-watch, and even as she did so a powerful copper-coloured Pontiac Firebird shot into sight as soundless and purposeful as a big cat. For some reason, quite irrational, Rosslyn took fright. She went back quickly to her desk, touching her fingers to her forehead as though an incipient headache lurked there, which in fact it did not. Her heart was vibrating within its narrow rib cage and she began to wonder at her curious reaction.

The sight of a very expensive and glamorous GT wasn't a very satisfactory reason. Perhaps it was the barren nature of the situation. According to Kylie, her father was forever in orbit, out of bounds, a man who found his own inner vision infinitely more intoxicating than anything before him, and Kylie usually illustrated and demonstrated her anecdotes from home. They showed a distressing lack of familial togetherness. The trouble appeared to be that Derek Ballinger could not have his artistic life complicated with child management and Sonia Ballinger was inevitably and more properly involved with having a good time and inhaling a great deal of overseas air. It was the classic situation of the poor little rich girl, and as far as Rosslyn could judge it was just as uncompromisingly accurate as Kylie said, even allowing for the child's natural flair for rhetoric and dramatics. The sweetest words a child ever knew, in simple terms the winged words of mutual love and involvement, Kylie apparently had never heard. Now after eight years of mismanagement and the child's own brave show degenerating into problem social attitudes, it was the parents, in Rosslyn's view, who needed shock treatment.

Two slams. Two people. So far no one had materialized. It was the voice she heard first, and even then it was profoundly revealing. It had the power to fascinate, crisply exact yet provocative, unshakably arrogant, distractingly attractive. It explained quite a lot, Rosslyn thought dismally. It possessed a dark, potent charm. Poor little Kylie! It would be quite something to have to live with that voice. A voice one would listen to, always. Whether that was a virtue or a vice, Rosslyn couldn't decide. Either way, one couldn't buy it or bottle it, and even an eight-year-old girl wouldn't be immune. The thought that this interview mightn't go as planned immediately crystallized. She wasn't going to be able to talk down to, or alternatively chat up, Derek Ballinger – that much was apparent. The extraordinary thing was that Kylie should dare to disregard that voice. Rosslyn herself viewed such a prospect with alarm. Just the sound of Derek Ballinger was disturbing her extremely, as though she was surrendering herself by the minute to such charming, brook-no-way-but-my-own arrogance. He didn't sound in the least like a visionary, but a man of action.

Now, alongside, Kylie's clear treble came piping

through. 'Oh, good, she's waited! I knew she would!'

Rosslyn stood up, firmly grasping the edges of the table. Right until the moment they appeared, man and child, she thought she had a chance. The world tilted gently to one side and her soft, very sweet, faintly husky voice just managed 'Good afternoon!' It sounded almost a question.

Far from looking the slightly inhuman monster of creativity, Derek Ballinger directed an indulgent, protective tenderness glance at Kylie's vivid, uplifted face. 'Go and play on the swings,' he said briefly, and Kylie did just that, after a knowing, conspiratorial wink at Rosslyn as though she was the one who was to be hauled over the coals as illogically she was feeling.

Derek Ballinger came forward as though Rosslyn's wide-eyed stare was done to a turn. 'Miss Marshall?'

Soundlessly she put out her hand. It was a beautiful hand and he took it, looking down at it in a sharply amused fashion. Anyone less like an abstracted intro-verted artist it would be difficult to imagine. The very air crackled about him with some overspill of some dark, matchless energy. Not in one million light years could Rosslyn see him space-watching. He had a quite extraordinary aura of vitality about him and she could feel the shock of it drumming right through to her fragile bones. Even when he dropped her hand the tingle of electricity lingered and her eyes began to lose themselves in the details of his face.

He was easily the most interesting-looking man she had ever seen, very tall with a powerful, lean frame and a kind of throw-away perfection about him that she took to be the easy and inevitable stamp of success. Here was no would-be-if-I-could-be, but the real thing, and she had the instant, unnerving sensation that the whole structure of this proposed meeting was about to fall apart.

'Why the desperate expression?' he asked in a casual, amused tone that was as slashing as a sword fight. His mouth was deeply moulded, his chin cleft, and his eyes that had the fire and flash of opals suddenly turned a metallic green.

'I'm sorry!' Inadequately she tried to rally. 'Please sit down, Mr. Ballinger. May I say how much I appreciate your coming.'

If she was studying him, he was studying her in a much more leisurely but well practised fashion. 'Nervous work, interviews, Miss Marshall?' he asked in a voice which was quite uninquisitive. 'I must apologize for being so late, but I only flew in this morning.'

'That's quite all right, Mr. Ballinger. I didn't mind waiting, and I did want to meet you.'

'While I thought Kylie was only *inventing* you!' He drew up a chair and looked about him with an instantly recognizable air of disparagement and a hint that he was going to drop any number of suggestions. 'What a particularly hideous room this is! I quite see why Kylie might want to change it!' His deeply bronzed skin had a gold glimmer to it and he looked very polished and civilized, his eyes the deep blue of turquoise shot with tiny slivers of green. The whole effect was electric until Rosslyn began to realize that the provocation in their brilliant depths wasn't being directed at her but at women in general. At once she felt antagonism begin to stir in her as though she was being patronized, or worse, laughed at.

'Unfortunately that kind of thing has repercussions, Mr. Ballinger,' she pointed out sweetly. 'In any case, it was the Activities Centre Kylie took the mind to paint!'

'Good God!' he said forcibly, 'then spare me the Concert Hall! Might I say only you look so separate from this dreary environment I might take a turn at painting myself. Wherever are the Building Fund's resources being channelled? But never mind. Kylie told me about your beautiful, dreamy face!'

For a moment Rosslyn looked utterly hazy, as well she might. 'Why, Mr. Ballinger, I'm not dreamy at all! I'm quite active where the wellbeing of my pupils is concerned, and I believe I'm a good teacher.'

'Very likely,' he said lazily, as though it was of no great importance. 'I'm quite sure you're excellent and you must enjoy all the heady excitement of school life – the atmosphere, the intrigue, the overtones, pupils like Kylie. It must never be lonely. What does strike me as bizarre is to find a genuine Renaissance beauty rooted in such a setting. Not that you're not still very much in embryo, which I suppose is a blessing!'

'But you're extraordinary!' she said faintly, feeling the shock of this fantastic man.

'Like Kylie!' he agreed, and smiled at her rather moodily. 'Still, I have a great respect for her taste and judgment. Needless to say, I was quite eager to gaze upon her heroine. You don't look much more than a child yourself. Even your voice is a young voice, not yet a woman's. Are you sure you're not some colourful captive of Miss Keating's?'

'If you'll allow me, Mr. Ballinger, as you're Kylie's father . . .'

He swung his head and sunlight fell over his dark, sardonic face. 'Miss Marshall,' he said dryly, 'I can hardly bring myself to tell you I'm not Kylie's father at all. I'm her uncle, Boyd Ballinger, ma'am!'

'How inexcusable!' she said, her golden eyes widening, reflecting the light.

'Don't be ridiculous, though I can see you're nervous and I'm making allowances. Derek is my brother — *stepbrother,* if we're going to split hairs. He really should have been here. He has a heart of gold, but his work is simply more dear to him than anything else. Professionally speaking, of course, it would have been well worth his visit. He would be fascinated with you. You have the rarest kind of colouring — very softly seductive, I believe it's called. Different textures and their handling have always had a remarkable appeal for Derek. You know the sort of thing — skin and hair, silk and satin. A study perhaps in tender creamy gold and rose amber. Would that be the colour of your hair? I'm not terribly knowledgeable about these matters.'

'Really,' she smiled, and her golden eyes glinted topaz; 'I thought you must be an artist yourself, Mr. Ballinger?'

'No way!' he cut her off a shade curtly. 'I'm what's popularly known as a cattle baron even in these days of crisis within the industry. Black Baron Ballinger to my enemies, and I have a few. There's nothing to stop my being a collector, of course, and I do wish you'd stop staring at me with those enormous almond eyes. I never permit a woman to look at me like that. There's a whole world of reproof in them, and there shouldn't be. At considerable inconvenience to myself I've come all the way out here to discuss my niece's progress, or lack of it. I thought she enjoyed her studies. In some departments, she's excellent. She described you to a T, but I put a lot of it down to her being an incurable romantic even at eight! Now it seems she knows a great deal about a lot of things.'

'But to be practical,' she pointed out, 'aren't we straying from the whole point of this meeting?'

'Allow me to contradict you, Miss Marshall, *I'm* not. You may be dithering a little because you've got a quick sketch of yourself gratis. The thing is, *I* know and *you* know, Kylie has a different home set-up from most children. Good or bad, it's the way it is. Why Derek married at all none of us have yet decided. It must have seemed a good idea at the time. Essentially he's a loner, but he does love Kylie in his way.'

'I hope so, Mr. Ballinger,' Rosslyn said fervently. 'Love is vital to the young.'

'It's vital to everyone, Miss Marshall, and you as solemn as a baby. How old are you, anyway?'

'I'm twenty-two, Mr. Ballinger,' she said tersely.

'I won't lose sight of that.' His voice slowed to a drawl. 'Why do you play down your looks? Never mind, I suppose you might have to. The mind boggles at what you might look like with a little more practice. Now, this has been an awfully long day for me. In the absence of Sonia, and Derek never does attend to these mundane matters, Kylie passed on to me your little note. I found it charming, diplomatic, touching, full of an earnest tenderness. I know you have Kylie's best interests at heart. Small wonder the child waxes lyrical about darling Miss Marshall, the one female in this establishment who isn't an ogre. Of course I might add you were born beautiful and you're very much one of the younger set. It appeals to innocent imaginations.'

'May I ask a question, Mr. Ballinger?' Rosslyn said courteously. 'Do you like me? I mean, do you think I'm good enough to be teaching your niece? There's such a thing as learning by listening, and you seem to be implying that Kylie only likes looking!'

'Well, I can hardly blame her for that. I do myself. No, set your mind at rest, Miss Marshall, I have the greatest confidence in your ability to mould the minds of the young. You see before you a convert. What I propose to do is this: when the school breaks up in what?'

'Two weeks.'

'—I intend taking Kylie back with me to Belyando. For the uninitiated, that's my property up in the Gulf country. I know all you're doubtless trying to explain to me, but what I want you to do for me, for Kylie, is this. Spend your vacation with her. Help her and train her. Give her the kind of companionship she needs. You know quite well she's very precocious and she doesn't mix all that well with her own age group. Naturally I would pay you and pay you well, though I can see you're disgusted with the sound of money. I wouldn't ask you to do it for nothing. Otherwise the deal's off.'

'Heavens, Mr. Ballinger,' Rosslyn protested, 'I didn't even know a deal was *on*! Conversing with you is like being carried along on a great tide.'

'Well, I usually get what I want,' he amended. 'Now don't cut adrift. Are you with me? You're the most ethereal-looking creature I've ever seen, but I'd hate to upset you.'

'Not at all! This is the most interesting discussion, but I can't believe it's real.'

'Perhaps you're tired,' he said suavely, and beneath that dark glitter of devilry was an underlying amusement. 'Tell me, have you anything planned for your vacation? Some glamorous sea trip?'

'It isn't merely a question . . .'

'*Tell* me!' he said in a hard, very calculating fashion, and she lifted her head, feeling the prickle of antagonism. It showed in her luminous eyes.

'I thought I might go to Ayars Rock!'

'Impenetrable in the hot season. A tea-rose like you would just shrivel up.'

'Some of my friends have made one or two suggestions.'

'And I've made a better one. Don't you want to help Kylie?'

'Of course I do!' she said in her sweet, husky voice. 'But I mean, can *you* make all these decisions—'

'Miss Marshall!' he drawled, and smiled. 'Forget that aspect of the case. I've been making decisions for a very long time. That's what makes me such an arrogant beast to your sweet little mind. It will be marvellous conversing with you, at any rate, or have you a cold coming on? I hope not. Your voice is very distinctive, sweetly demure as a crinoline. Kylie is very fond of you. She would be thrilled to hear you're coming along.'

'What about her parents?' Rosslyn said patiently.

'Oh, Derek would be thrilled too. I don't know about Sonia. Perhaps you'd better bring along a pair of spectacles.'

There was a tremendous alertness about him for all the elegant indolence of his lean body. She studied him thoughtfully with a faint trace of melancholy that was quite unconscious and fairly habitual to her expression. He laughed outright.

'Why, you seem to be treating me as a joke!' she flashed at him.

'My dear girl!' his opal-tinted eyes flashed over her. 'You inspire me with the greatest respect. It's asking rather a lot, I know, to give all the pleasure trips you're set upon, but Belyando is a gift, believe me, and I know Kylie's best interests are very dear to your heart. I wouldn't expect money to interest you, but allow me to recompense you for my own satisfaction. Well?'

'Perhaps,' she said a little distractedly as though she was being led along a way she didn't wish to go.

'It's about time you worked up a little enthusiasm. Belyando is not a simple cottage in the country. If you come I promise I'll line up all sorts of exciting activities suitable for a gently bred girl. Do you ride?'

'No,' she said firmly, shaking her rose-amber head. 'I've never even seen a horse at close range.'

'You're joking!' He tilted back precariously in his chair, speaking in tones of the liveliest interest.

'No,' she said calmly, *and think what you like about that!*

His beautiful white teeth snapped together and he righted his chair. 'Comical or not, you can be taught, Miss Marshall. I'm sure I'd be delighted to find the time and you can take a few lessons just to please me. Now why look at me as though you find that hard to believe! You really should, as a teacher, begin to guard your expressions. So far I've seen a thousand and one and a lot of amazed scorn. It's not the look I prefer in women.'

'Of course not!' she said quickly, then clamped her mouth shut on the reckless desire to say more. It seemed to her his turquoise blue eyes with their sunburst of gold and green flecks were goading her on to the very brink of damnation. A twist of diablerie appeared to be common to both Kylie and her uncle. Nevertheless she was ashamed of herself. 'Forgive me,' she said softly, 'that was impertinent!'

'Yes. But you couldn't resist it. Oddly enough, I admire candour, at a first meeting. I dare say I can expect big things from you in the near future.'

Her ear was attuned to all the nuances in his voice, every last one of them disturbing. 'You seem to be talking down to me, Mr. Ballinger. It puts me at a slight

19

disadvantage.'

'Well, you just toss that thought away right now. It's not intentional, believe me. Now that you mention it I feel rather helpless myself. Take heart from it. Perhaps the feeling is mutual?'

'I don't think so!' She stood up, certain now he was only mock-serious.

He stood up as well, with his lithe swinging challenge, inevitably towering over her, his sparkling slightly cynical eyes moving with precision all over her, adding up her simple outfit, the rust-coloured ten-dollar skirt, the five-dollar deep yellow shirt that still made her face glow like a flower. He even touched on her sandals which just happened to cost much more than the skirt and blouse put together and his dark face glittered with a cool, masculine amusement.

'You're being very decisive, Miss Marshall. Do I take it the meeting's over?'

She had to tilt her head to look up at him. 'Not at all, Mr. Ballinger. It's simply that I've been sitting down for the most part of the day.'

'Half your luck!' he commented laconically. 'I've been to two conferences black with insults across the table. Do you blame me if I find the sight of you distractingly refreshing? I'm very old-fashioned about women, Miss Marshall. Almost Victorian. I like them as ornaments.'

'How disgustingly chauvinistic!'

'I admit it,' he said blandly. 'No use looking to me for support for Women's Lib. I just like a woman to look pretty and turn out a good meal.'

'Is that the lot?' she asked incredulously. 'You can't be serious!'

'I'm doing my best, though I have to admit those enormous golden eyes of yours are egging me on. Of course, Miss Marshall, you're quite right. That's only the broad picture. Actually I do like a few other things besides.'

The look in his eyes, the unholy satire of his voice almost rooted her to the spot. His appearance if anything was even more significant for her than his voice. She felt totally deprived of all her usual good sense as though the sight of him only confirmed her initial sense of inability to cope with the situation. She would have to come to terms with all her flustered feelings before confronting Boyd Ballinger on his home grounds. Extrovert, egoist, supreme male, and so attractive she didn't like to think about it.

'You must have been a fearful child!' she volunteered, trying to regain her poise.

'I can see you're dying to say like Kylie!'

'Worse than Kylie, I should say, and I didn't mean that at all. I *like* Kylie!'

'Thank you. If you had said you liked me I wouldn't have believed you, but be that as it may, are you coming to Belyando? Kylie would consider it a miracle! I feel bound to add I see it in that light myself!'

'Is it possible I'm dreaming all this?' She felt quite confused, flashing him rather emotion-laden glances. 'I suppose if I said no, you'd contrive to bend my mind?'

'I'm not prepared to say with what method, but yes,

I think so. There's no need to feel sorry for yourself, you'll have a wonderful time. If you're never going to make an equestrienne, I suppose you do hold a driving licence?'

'Mine is the little Datsun you've put to shame,' she pointed out dryly.

'Well, of course I wouldn't expect a little dream girl like you to be in charge of a Firebird.'

'I could drive it,' she said recklessly, flicked by his arrogant presumption that she couldn't.

'And there'll be no way you'll be put to the test, so silence all the protests. Now, this I'll do for you instead. I'll chat up Kylie and she'll listen. In fact I wouldn't be surprised if you don't have a model child on your hands at least until the school vacation. Then you can do the rest. I'll tell the family of my plans and they'll fall in with them.'

'Are you sure?' she couldn't resist asking.

'They always do,' he said, and she believed him profoundly. 'Derek and Sonia live in considerable style, and it doesn't all come from the paintings, you know.'

'Oh.' She made a funny little grimace of complete comprehension.

'So I would be most grateful to you, Rosslyn – may I? – if you tell your family and all your friends that you've decided to do the proper thing and help a small child find herself. I could see at a glance that you're extremely loyal, not to say tender-hearted. Perhaps a little *too* tender-hearted now that I examine you more thoroughly. I'm a bit of an authority on such things.'

'Could it be the light failing, do you think? Actually I'm quite spunky, Mr. Ballinger!'

'Boyd, please!' he insisted. 'I know I didn't say so before, but you may call me Boyd. I'm sure you're spunky, Rosslyn, to use your own funny little word from the gym, but surely one can be tender and spunky at the same time?'

'I'm sure you know I'm no match for you, Mr. Ballinger.'

'Give yourself time. You must be tired after a long week at school. If the Boyd doesn't come easily to your tongue, it will fairly soon. *Mr.* Ballinger was reserved for my father. A good many of the staff were the friends of my childhood. I grew up with them. They taught me how to ride the wild horses, to cut cattle, bushcraft, the lot. I'm Boyd to everyone until they step out of line, then I'm Mr. Ballinger for as long as it takes. Even a cattle baron can't demand too much formality when a station is a whole kingdom in itself. The house girls and the piccaninnies usually call me Miz Boyd, which is fascinating, otherwise the Miz Boyd is completely unknown.'

She was gazing at him with all the soft, intent curiosity of a kitten, in turn vaguely mesmerizing him with her fixed, almond-eyed stare. 'But *you* can always call me Boyd,' he continued, and smiled as though he found her strangely intriguing, as she was very different in a sense. 'Now look here,' he said with such briskness she almost jumped, 'I must break the bad news. I have to go. I know between the two of us we're going to work wonders with Kylie, but I haven't had the opportunity to have that pep talk with her as yet. God knows what manner of mischief she might be getting into at the moment!'

Rosslyn came back to the present with something of an effort. She usually managed much better and she would be covered in confusion afterwards, but that was the effect he had upon her. She whirled around, looking worried, staring out into the grounds as though Boyd Ballinger could see something she couldn't. 'I'll come with you,' she said, looking back at him a bit helplessly. 'The caretaker will lock up the classroom!'

'Good! Well, come along, then. One must put a foot right some part of the day, and you're my only victory to date.'

'Victory?' she questioned him with her first show of real spirit.

'I'm sorry, I really am. How tactless! Never mind what I say, Rosslyn. What does it matter?' He stood for a moment looking down at her, well over six feet, looking all the things he really was; rich and powerful and probably relentless, the attitude of his lean body very devil-may-care-but-I-don't. 'What a fantastically pretty girl you are, Rosslyn,' he said in a calm, professional voice like an antique dealer. 'Women are terrifying really. There's so much more to them than a man might suspect. I could stand here and watch you all day, but there's time enough for that. I want you to promise me you'll stay on Belyando and make a job of it!'

Her winged eyebrows flew up in surprise. 'It may be

a very brave thing I'm doing – and I don't mean Kylie!' Try as she did, she couldn't see behind all the sparkling mockery.

'*Promise me!*' he said, his voice taut as wire.

'All right! I'll do it, of course.'

'Good girl. And you're pleased?'

'I'm thrilled!' she said, not untruthfully.

'I knew quite well you would be, but I wanted to make sure!'

She flushed a little at the glimmer of laughter in his gem-coloured eyes. 'I suppose manipulating a mere schoolteacher is easy?'

'Child's play!' he agreed. 'Now don't go all feminine on me. I'm going to persist in seeing you as an enchanting child not all that much different from Kylie!'

'How foolish!' she murmured, saying the first thing that came into her head.

'Yes, isn't it?' His eyes rested on her face for a moment, very thoroughly and rather broodingly. 'You're not trying to flirt with me, are you, Rosslyn?'

'I wouldn't dare. I mean, I wouldn't dream of it. How presumptuous.' And how very difficult not to, she thought. Boyd Ballinger seemed to inspire that kind of thing, so that she had a tremendous awareness of herself as a woman.

'That being the case,' he said, sounding unconvinced, 'I'll think up all sorts of things a grateful uncle can devise.'

'You don't have to bother on my account!'

'It will be a pleasure! I can see you're a very lovable personality.'

'Like Kylie?'

'That's the girl!' He turned on her a turquoise green gaze that was utterly exasperating. 'That way we won't have any mishaps!'

The colour flooded her creamy gold skin. 'Whatever do you mean?'

'Rosslyn,' he said tersely, 'I'm not a man who wastes time, neither am I a marrying man. Got it?'

'Not only got it, I'm flattened! Why should you feel it encumbent upon yourself to tell *me*?'

'Rosie!' he said earnestly. 'The veriest bush baby could tell you bright colours in nature go hand in hand with danger. Besides, modesty forbids my telling you how many times I've been chased in the past. Of course it's not all me. Belyando has something to do with it!'

'Incredible! You're in absolutely no danger from me!'

'Which wasn't quite what I said. Now with you it could be the other way around. I suspect you're an enchantress, however much you're disguised as a schoolteacher, a throwback to the age of Romanticism. You'd be ravishing in the right dress.'

'I wouldn't be regarded very benevolently if I floated around here in drapes,' she said rather tartly.

'No, perhaps not. Now, where's Kylie?' He moved so quickly she was left looking after him. Hastily Rosslyn gathered up her things and chased after him, her hair in the sunlight flaring into riotous glowing life. She clapped her hands, calling 'Kylie!' but Kylie failed to appear.

'Perhaps she's sitting out some vigil in the school chapel? Boyd Ballinger suggested.

'More likely a paper massacre! What's got into her? This is silly. *Kylie?*' She began to call out again, running as though she could put off the possibility of Kylie's delving into mischief no longer.

Boyd Ballinger, without even appearing to move, cut off her momentum, his hand on her wrist with cool mastery, calling her back to attention as easily as any runaway filly. 'Whoa there! Shall we settle down? Kylie's in the car, asleep most probably. Do you know what hours that child keeps? I mean literally? Derek, when the muse is on him, just goes adrift, cloud seven, and Sonia is not used to spending her evenings at home.'

'Oh, truly, I didn't realize!' Rosslyn turned her glowing young face up to him, her short shining curls clustered like rose leaves about her head. 'I mean, I thought she went to bed!'

'She does!' he agreed, and gave an eloquent shrug. 'All in her own good time. About midnight, I think. Briefly, that's my case for taking her back to Belyando. The child needs her rest. She just lives on nervous energy. She'd got enormous potential, but she seems to be running wild. Quite frankly, I'm worried about her.'

'Well, that's a very good thing in your favour, Mr. Ballinger!' she said with the sweetest and most serious sincerity.

'Do I need good things in my favour, Miss School-teacher?' he mocked her.

'Certainly. I shouldn't say this, I know, you will in

some respects be my employer, though to be quite honest I'd much rather you didn't pay me anything at all. My board will be quite enough and I'm sure Belyando will be beautiful . . .'

He held up a hand to divert her. 'Forget all that. What really interests me is what *is* it you shouldn't say? The suspense is well nigh killing me.'

'Nothing. Let's drop it. I mustn't say it, I realize that now. It was a personal observation, and as we must be one big happy family together I'm not looking for trouble!'

'And just how, by the way, could you bring that on your pretty head?'

'I'm not sure,' she said honestly. 'It's just a feeling I have. I'm a bit psychic. Sometimes it's useful, other times it fills me with horror!'

The impulse to laugh became quite uncontrollable. He put back his head and Rosslyn found herself looking at the clean curve of his mouth. All the while, without realizing it, she appeared to be amusing him no end. He had a beautiful mouth, she could see, and very definite and interesting bone structure, the hard angle of his chin emphasized by the deep cleft in it.

'Please stop laughing at me,' she said. 'One gets rattled!'

'What about *me*? Ah well, better not delve into it. Now come along. I'll see you to your car.' His eyes licked over her, calculating, experimental, still brilliant with laughter. 'I don't suppose you'd care to have dinner with me?'

'Certainly not!' she said primly, from pure shock.

'And that's only smart, Miss Schoolteacher!' He caught her arm neatly, his darkly tanned face, behind the mock gravity, convulsed with laughter. 'I'm well over due for a set-down!'

'And I can see I'm going to have my patience tried to the limit if all you're going to do is laugh at me.'

'Goodness me, no. You have a strange effect on me, I'll admit, but you're over-simplifying my emotions. Small wonder Kylie loves you. Why, if I saw too much of you I'd go soft myself!'

A few feet away in the big Pontiac, Kylie suddenly sat up and paid attention, her sable waves decorated with daisies and wisps of grass, her large blue eyes full of concern and sleepy concentration. Not for the world would she have told anyone, but she had been shaking inside all day. Miss Marshall was so friendly and gentle and sweet and Uncle Boyd was as super an uncle as anyone could wish for; even so this day had seemed without end. The outcome of the late afternoon interview had secretly disturbed Kylie immensely. It struck her with a pang that she really cared about these two people – Miss Marshall and the Uncle Boyd she had wished over and over again was her own father.

Miss Marshall's hair in the sunlight looked like a whole kaleidoscope of magic bubbles: gold and amber and a flame pink rose, her luminous eyes set like a Persian kitten's all golden and glowing. To Kylie, who was extraordinarily susceptible to such things, Rosslyn looked indescribably lovely like a never-blossomed-before flower, trembling in the breeze. She was spring, and Kylie loved the spring. She jerked herself upright like a small puppet on a string, watching the man and the girl walking towards her. Miss Marshall looked oddly fragile and beautiful beside Uncle Boyd's very tall, strong-looking frame, his deep tan very marked, his eyes the exact colour of the opal in the pendant he had given her last Christmas. He had found the opal himself and that made the present all the more memorable.

The flowers and the lawns, the lavender blue glory of the jacarandas, the rather haphazard arrangement of the extra wings to the main school building which was very mellow and gracious, the moving figures in the foreground, all took on vivid detail for Kylie in a way she thought of as perfectly ordinary but was in fact a kind of phenomenon, for Kylie in her full maturity was to become a celebrated artist. Now, at eight, she had a critical faculty that was quite remarkable, a half realized talent, but an aversion to painting 'true' pictures like Daddy for the very reason that he never had time for her, always being occupied with some half painted canvas propped up on an easel. Her mother was like some bright, flashing vision, living the life of the fashionable rich, though it was seemingly Uncle Boyd's money, she had found out once from eavesdropping on an argument – or rather her mother was shouting and her father was predictably silent. They were people who lived untouched by one another, or so Kylie thought in her innocence. It was clear that both of them could live without her.

It was Miss Marshall who seemed to Kylie the most visually entrancing human creature she had ever laid eyes on except for Uncle Boyd, and he was quite different, very clearly a big strong man who towered over everybody, with a smile on his mouth and a light in his startlingly greenish blue eyes. Miss Marshall was a dream girl in an enchanted garden, like the illustration in a book of fairy stories someone had given her. Kylie checked her impulse to fling herself out of the car and demand to know what they had been talking about, then she saw Uncle Boyd smile and his beautiful sleek voice with a funny cutting edge to it came floating across to her, so matter-of-fact and unsensational it was almost as much protection as being taken by the hand.

'Kylie, get out of the car like a good girl. I have something important to tell you.'

She stared back at him stupefied for a moment, with the sudden splintering of fright, then she pushed out of the door and raced towards him, quite simply for reassurance. Miss Marshall just stood there smiling and the wild beating of Kylie's heart relaxed its accelerated pace. Everything was all right. She drew a shallow, choking breath of relief. She wasn't going to be put into some other sickening school where the teachers didn't understand one like Miss Marshall. Miss Marshall never shouted or grew angry or thought up a thousand and one little punishments. Even on the days when she ticked Kylie off she was very fair about it, so Kylie, on a wave of reaction, stretched out her hand to either of them.

'You can tell her if you like!' Uncle Boyd said in his charming, mocking voice, so Rosslyn, caught somewhere between man and child, bent down so that she was level with Kylie's gentian blue eyes.

'How would you like me to come to Belyando with you for the school vacation? Your Uncle Boyd said I might.'

Kylie's small face whitened visibly as it did when she cared intensely about something. She glanced at her uncle sharply, but he only nodded rather idly, contemplating the effect of the sunlight on Miss Marshall's hair. Then Kylie's face in front of them, like some wary small creature not wholly tame, began to break into smiles. These smiles grew with her expanding pleasure and excitement so that soon it broke out of bounds and Kylie, who despised and detested all manner of weeping and weakness, burst into tears, embracing Rosslyn in the boisterous fashion that reminded her uncle a good deal of a puppy being shown its new owner.

'Then it's congratulations all round!' he said gently. 'Life is good, full of surprises. Not one day can we count on running to plan. Kylie, I'm sure Miss Marshall appreciates your radiant appreciation, but sweetie, you're knocking her down!'

'I'm sorry, Miss Marshall!' Kylie drew back instantly, fastidiously flicking teardrops off her face. 'You've just made such a difference to me, that's all. It will be a wonderful holiday. Belyando is out of this world, and Uncle Boyd is terribly rich, you know!'

'A fact I'm at pains to conceal! Do stop, Kylie.'

'Maybe we could all go and have tea somewhere?' Kylie suggested, bent now on celebrating.

'There'll be plenty of other times,' Uncle Boyd said

lightly. 'Miss Marshall, my pet, has to go home. She has lots of packing to do – explaining.'

'Brilliant!' said Kylie, rapt. 'I can scarcely believe it. You've never done such a thing for me before, Uncle Boyd.'

'No. But then we've never known Miss Marshall. There is that distinction.'

'Yes, of course. Oh, I feel absolutely exalted!' Kylie fluted. 'I'll take good care, Miss Marshall, to behave. I promise!'

'I'm counting on that, Kylie!' Rosslyn smiled with the air of one who had every intention of holding her small charge to her promise. Certainly Kylie and her uncle sent out powerful radiations that were as marked as their family resemblance.

'I've never lied to you, have I, Uncle Boyd?' Kylie demanded. 'I'll behave.'

'Somewhat to my moderate surprise, I believe you. Really, honey, so don't save your breath up, you'll explode. Now, hold up your head. No more tears. Say good-bye to Miss Marshall and hop back into the car.'

In the most carefree way imaginable Kylie did both of these things. It was something of an occasion for her to be saying she was going to behave and meaning it! As a matter of fact she could have made up her long running feud with Miss George, which was as good a guide as any to her angelic state of mind.

'I'll wait until you go, Miss Marshall!' Boyd Ballinger said obligingly, except that his eyes deepened to green, a sure sign of his awful predilection for teasing.

'I can't say I'm any too happy about that!' Rosslyn said, falling back a step. 'I'll probably stall the engine or crash the gears, something I haven't done for years. You go first.'

'I understand!' he said smoothly. 'This has been a highly emotional afternoon. I have to go north again the day after tomorrow. I'll contact you further with my plans. I'll probably come back for you and Kylie myself. Derek and Sonia can make their own arrangements. Derek only cares to be airborne in spirit. He never flies if he can help it – strange for a Ballinger. However, I expect both of them for a good part of the stay. Derek has always worked very well on the property. Some of his best canvases have captured all the colour and light of the tropics. More accurately, I think he finds a certain peace there. After all, it's where he was born, and marriage, as anyone will tell you, is full of tremendous strains!'

'Not for you, I'm sure,' she said thoughtlessly.

'I've been a bachelor these many years and I've grown used to it.'

'There's always the moment, Mr. Ballinger, when nothing other than marriage is possible.'

'Surely you're not thinking in terms of a shotgun affair. Where's your finesse, Miss Marshall?'

'What's got into you two?' Kylie called from the car.

'It's all right, pet,' Boyd Ballinger comforted her. 'Miss Marshall and I are entitled to our significant discussions in depth. It's all part of the game!'

'You'd better stand away from the car, Miss Marshall!' Kylie warned her. 'Uncle Boyd usually shuts his eyes when he reverses!'

Swiftly Rosslyn returned the man's smile. She looked into his eyes and for a moment there was no sound but the steady drum of her heart. Her eyes dropped to the curve of his mouth, then her heavy lashes came down on her cheeks. She was afraid to look at him any more. She moved back as quick and neat as a humming bird in full retreat. All her pulses had turned volcanic. The sun caught her eyes, dazzling her, and she threw up a protective hand. Perhaps she had acted rashly, but the deed was done now. Certainly she had decided for the most pure of motives.

Kylie *did* need her, yet she had never felt before as she did now. Almost as though she had won some overwhelming prize she wouldn't know what to do with anyhow. She would go to Belyando, and all the rest of it was in the hands of Boyd Ballinger!

CHAPTER TWO

THREE weeks later Rosslyn flew into the Far Northern empire the Ballingers had built for themselves. She had never seen anything like it. From the air it looked like a small settlement nestling into a densely green valley, sunlit and hill-shadowed. On the ground, it would seem to her immense. Like the rest of the big cattle stations, Belyando had suffered its share of setbacks with the falling beef market, but unlike the great drought-ridden stations of the south-west well over a thousand miles away, Belyando lay well within the monsoonal belt. The previous year had proved cyclonic, with record floods all over the vast State of Queensland; now in this holding good season, Belyando's beauty was breathtaking.

The earth had revived itself with prodigal lavishness, for this was the best time to see the tropics, on the verge of the Wet. The great trees began to blossom, the magnificent poincianas, the tulip trees and the jacarandas, the yellow blossoming cascara trees, the brilliant parasite, the bougainvillea, that laced itself everywhere, smothering the landscape in drifts of crimson and white and purple. It was lush, vital country, with a rich volcanic soil, bright red beneath the thickly grassed savannahs and the luxuriant spear-grass that stood breast-high. Changing larkspur mountains, now blue, now purple, dominated the skyline and great chains of billabongs flashed like silver ribbons until they reached the impenetrable rain forest, true rain jungle, and beyond broad winding rivers and croco-dile-infested swamps their mirror-greenness massed with exquisite blue and ivory lotus lilies that sat on their plump green pads, the perfect concealment for the unspeakably hideous monsters of the mud. Such was the tropic North, the Ballingers' place in the sun, and they had been developing it extensively for well over a century.

With the State capital, Brisbane, nearly two thou-sand miles away from its furthest tip, Cape York, the long trip up the Coast had been an eternal succession of green: the great canefields, the pineapple plantations, the pawpaw groves, the tea and tobacco plantations. It was like looking down at a giant salad bowl. Now the land was given over to cattle, grazing by the thousands, and the *birds*! Great flights of black and white ibis and the blue cranes, the brolgas, the black swans and the tens of thousands of wild duck and the magpie geese that stalked the magnificent lagoons that ran into a network of swamps where the crocodile lay and swamp pythons slithered their twenty feet or more into the emerald flower-decked water where the jabiru and spi-dery-legged water birds just missed brutal jaws. Beyond the limits of the station was a vast tropical jungle, making it easy for Rosslyn to realize that once every section of Ballinger land had been heavily tim-bered. For many long years the cleared pastures had been sown from the ground. Now it was done by air, and enormous capital had been poured into clearing the rain forest and developing new breeds of cattle that stood up to the humid climate of the tropics, the Zebus, the Brahmans and the Santa Gertrudis. Only a year before the pilot of a Pawnee agricultural plane had been killed on the property when his light aircraft hit the tops of some trees.

For Rosslyn it was sobering and fascinating at the same time to look down on this seemingly inaccessible spot, surrounded by dense rain forest that sprang up almost as quickly as it was cleared. For most of the trip, Kylie had chatted non-stop, but for more than a half hour since Boyd Ballinger had radioed that they were on their way in, her glossy head had lolled back in sleep. Now before them, the all-weather landing strip ran out in a precise glittery grey path through the blaze of brilliant green. The hangar roof flashed silver, dazzling Rosslyn's eyes, but she had other things to think about. Like her stomach. She had flown in a Boeing 707, but it was a different type of travel from a Cherokee Six for all its limousine comfort.

A savage kind of panic held her in thrall. It was terrifying and as hard to control as an attack of claustrophobia. They were coming in fast with a brisk tail wind and she could have shrieked aloud. As a pilot Boyd Ballinger could hardly have been bettered, but she had gone beyond the point of appreciating all that. Her sensations were purely physical; her fingernails dragged into the skin of her palms. The fine blaze of colour seemed to be rushing towards them, the great shade trees flaming scarlet that lined the track, the grey strip and the white buildings, the figures on the ground with their faces upturned. He could not possibly have guessed how she felt. Kylie was awake now, as chirrupy and excited as a crimson chat.

It was no laughing matter. Rosslyn was literally paralysed with fright, as she looked out over the wings that seemed to be lifting up and down like a great gull's. Flying with the Ballingers might be routine, but for that moment she fervently wished she had been left behind. She couldn't even think of a few prayers, just this queer passive acceptance that the trip might prove fatal. Her reaction to the rushing sensation of homing in marked her down as a novice, and she had the certain notion she might never get used to it.

Beside her, Boyd Ballinger looked as unconcerned as if it was a jeep he was nosing into a parking spot. The handling of a plane and a jeep were probably much the same thing to him, but Rosslyn had no confidence at all – not in him, not in her. He couldn't set the plane down lightly. They were going to pitch in on a cross wind and there would probably be an inquiry. One read of these light aircraft crashes all the time. She writhed under her seat belt and put her head back, lying still. One thing he couldn't say was she was trying to distract him by chatting. Kylie suddenly caught sight of Miss Marshall's fatalistic face and broke into belated words of sympathy and encouragement, but Rosslyn was braced for the worst.

It didn't happen. They put down as lightly as a blue crane racing into the river flats, but even then Rosslyn couldn't stop her convulsive swallowing. She heard Kylie's voice urgently inquiring after her health, then

Boyd Ballinger's amused, faintly impatient drawl:

'You're easily the most nervous passenger I've ever had. Relax, child, the worst phase is over!'

'Yes, Miss Marshall,' Kylie said kindly, 'we're on the ground!'

'I have no desire to find out!'

'Would you rather I carried you?' Boyd Ballinger suggested.

Rosslyn neither answered nor changed her expression, which was one of breathless martyrdom.

'No takers?' he asked, and laughed. 'Kylie, I've dropped the steps. You can hop out.'

'Do you want me to go?' Kylie said.

'That's what I asked. Come on now, Rosslyn, this kind of thing is rather dampening. You can't sit around when everyone has turned out to meet you. There's quite a welcoming committee outside!'

Rosslyn opened her eyes which were enormous and dazed. 'Am I supposed to give a speech? If so, I don't think I could manage it!'

'Let the speech pass,' he suggested. 'Just get out and look beautiful.'

'I'm sorry. I realize I'm something else again from what you're used to.'

'I never make comparisons, Miss Marshall,' he said, with a certain wry amusement. 'Here, shall I help you?'

He reached across and unflipped her seat belt, put one hand out and lifted her to her feet. Her legs were trembling and she wished only to get out into the fresh air. 'All right,' she said, 'you go ahead!'

40

'As long as you're coming!' he said, his eyes on her delicate, rather melancholy face . . .

'Of course!' Her vision, usually twenty-twenty, was cloudy like a fog before her eyes. She fastened her eyes on a point somewhere between his broad shoulders and followed him down the wide centre aisle, knowing well enough she wanted to flake out.

Then the danger was real. Boyd was on the ground looking up at her, his arms reaching for her waist, obviously not trusting her to the stairs. His opal-coloured eyes were all blue and green and gold jostling fires, the tautness of his expression giving his thoughts away.

'I think I'm going to . . .'

'Faint,' he said in a hard, meaningful way, and took her full slight weight as she came falling towards him. 'Damn!'

'It happens all the time!' Kylie called out, vastly distracted by the whole thing.

'Not to me it doesn't!' her uncle said. 'I can't afford the time. Back, the lot of you,' he said in his Big Boss manner that instantly got results; the welcoming committee were struck dumb with surprise.

In the shade, Rosslyn stirred within seconds and opened her eyes. They looked utterly lost, her creamy gold skin almost paled to porcelain.

'So I was right!' Boyd Ballinger said tonelessly. 'I knew the moment I saw you were different!'

'I fainted.'

'Right before our eyes!'

'I'm sorry,' she whispered.

'Don't talk!' he said rather curtly. 'I'll get you up to

41

the house. You're only a featherweight, so I'll carry you over to the station waggon.'

'I can walk, I mean it,' she protested, looking incapable of anything.

'*Please*. I know you want to walk, but I don't want to have to pick you up off the ground again. Just remember, I always know best!'

'Yes, he does!' Kylie seconded, in wonder at all these strange happenings. 'Is this the first time you've fainted, Miss Marshall?'

'No,' Rosslyn said, somewhat reluctantly. 'I used to as a child.'

'Oh, for God's sake!' Boyd Ballinger moved swiftly, picking Rosslyn up like the featherweight he claimed she was. 'Fill Kylie in later with tales of your early days. Right now, I'm getting you up to the house before your eyes swamp your whole face.'

'We all react differently,' Kylie pointed out in a highly clinical manner. 'I'm usually violently ill myself. I remember . . .'

'I'm a man of considerable patience, Kylie, but you understand how it is with me,' her uncle said. 'Enough is enough! I love you, but don't make things any more difficult for me.'

'No, Uncle Boyd. I'll just get in the back and hold Miss Marshall's hand.'

'Call me Rosslyn!' Rosslyn suggested. 'Seeing we're friends, and we're both staying with your uncle. You can't keep on with the Miss Marshall. It seems out of place now.'

'Oh, lovely, thank you, Rosslyn. Such a lovely name.

It reminds me of a flower. Uncle Boyd thinks so too. An apricot tea-rose, he said.'

'I thought we discussed that in confidence,' Boyd Ballinger said.

'Yes!' Kylie agreed, smiling. 'But you never said I couldn't tell!'

'Flying! I can't pretend I'll ever enjoy it!' Rosslyn sighed.

'You'll have to learn how to.'

'I couldn't. I'm not built for it.'

'Forget it,' he said, looking into her face so close to his shoulder. 'Later on, I'll prove that you can. For now, you can wave to the staff. They've been waiting around for a large part of the afternoon, I'll bet.'

'Good grief! They must think I'm a cream puff!'

'*Well*, at least you're extraordinarily attractive!'

'I feel much better now, thank you. You could put me down.'

'Am I asking for orders? I give them out here, girl. And that piece of information is particularly important where you're concerned.'

A million pulses were hammering under her thin skin, and she had the most tremendous impulse to touch his face, a kind of madness generated by his close proximity. He caught her looking at him and his expression brought the colour into her face.

'Flutter your hand and be charming, but don't go wanting what you can't have!'

For a moment she felt quite stricken, as though he read every thought in her head, then she began to wave at the welcoming party with much delicacy and charm.

It seemed to make a wonderful difference. Boyd Ballinger's foreman, a few of his trusted hands, some of the house girls, the lubras, a whole swarm of piccaninnies, and one very ancient and formidable-looking old gin suddenly caught fire, turning the homecoming into something spectacular, waving and bowing in the most exhilarated fashion, the piccaninnies clapping their hands, their great liquid black eyes melting with smiles.

Rosslyn found it very funny and very touching.

'How's that?' Kylie asked. 'You see, they liked you.'

'Some welcome! I'm sorry I had to go fluttery and spoil everything.'

'Don't apologize,' Boyd Ballinger said dryly, something not quite a smile in his eyes. 'I think you've impressed them. It's really turned out quite an occasion and the children have never seen anyone with your colour hair. A very convincing piece of woman magic.'

'Red-gold hair is very ordinary, surely?'

'Never! It's a phenomenon out here, and *your* colour hair would be noticed anywhere, as I'm sure you very well know.'

'I'm not deliberately looking for compliments, Mr. Ballinger.'

'Sure, I know. But you got one!' His eyes went that metallic green again and his hold on her tightened.

Her hand on his shoulder visibly trembled and Kylie took this to be a manifestation of hunger. 'You'll be much better after you've had something to eat,' she said stoutly. 'I'll run on ahead and open the car doors.'

'All right?' Boyd Ballinger asked Rosslyn as he lowered her into the seat.

'Yes, I'm fine, now, thank you.'

'And a good thing!' He shut the door firmly on her side and got into the driver's seat, calling out to his foreman to taxi the Cherokee into the hangar and give him an hour.

Rosslyn in the back seat tried to will herself back into calm self-possession. She could still feel his hard, inflexible arms around her. He probably thought her the most foolish young woman he had ever met. Her glowing curls made a mist around her head and she turned her small face with its wide, tilted eyes towards the welcoming party, beginning to wave again. Kylie, from the other window, did the same, with the splendid detached arrogance of Royalty. The Ballingers were born to this kind of thing, but Rosslyn, by a sheer fluke, she thought, made the most of the occasion, lending it a considerable amount of grace. Clearly they found her faint entrancing and perhaps for the coloured people it had some magic omen, like her rose-fire curls. No one could say her arrival had been dull, and therein, she supposed, lay her triumph. With so little outside entertainment available in this lovely remote place she was bound to score a hit.

Boyd Ballinger caught her eyes in the rear vision mirror and the moment had a curious intimacy which disturbed Rosslyn extremely. Still she smiled at him, a very sweet, genuinely grateful smile that was reflected in her large golden eyes, but he glanced away from her abruptly. Probably he thought she was a creature quite foreign to him, and Rosslyn thought so too. Beside her Kylie was giving some jovial little pantomime for the benefit of the piccaninnies, who adored a joke, her vivid little face in the incredible blaze of sunlight as soft and frank as a pansy. She looked as she was meant to look, happy and carefree, not tense and wilful, seizing the reins of the class. Then they were away and Kylie began to point out all the landmarks and places of interest on the very pleasant drive back to the house.

'We're going to have such a wonderful time!' she enthused. 'Oh, boy, am I glad to be here! That stuffy old Morlands is the most miserable place ever,' she said, feeling a remembered flash of rage. 'But this is different!' she breathed. 'This is beautiful. The most beautiful place in the world.'

'A proper little bushwhacker is Kylie,' her uncle said, and smiled.

'I don't blame her!' Rosslyn murmured, her mind fully occupied with sights and scents and sounds. But it was too brief a glimpse. She wanted days, weeks, to explore. Her mind seemed obsessed with colour, the flamboyant scarlet of an immense avenue of poincianas, the native trees stuck with all kinds of coloured berries, the pink and the purple of the bougainvillea that burned along the fences and completely covered the roof and the sides of one whitewashed building, the heat and the low-hung radiant sun. The whole atmosphere was so persuasive, so redolent of all she had ever read of the tropics, she began to fall under its spell. This

46

was a big man's country, brilliant and rather turbulent. Lonely too. Station people had to be special.

They were sweeping past a beautiful, pandanus-fringed lagoon and the birds rose up all around them. It was the most fascinating sight, a black frieze moving like flame against the cobalt sky.

'I've never seen so many birds!' she breathed.

'There must be tens of thousands of them,' Kylie said most intelligently. 'You must see the brolgas dance. They're wonderful. It's like a real ritual and they have set steps, the loveliest I've ever seen. Mrs. Morrison would be an old hippopotamus beside the brolgas.'

Rosslyn turned to answer, but her attention was caught by a great blaze of purple convolvulus that trailed down a bloodwood in a mighty sweep. Such a sight filled her with an intense sensuous pleasure. She flung out her arm towards Kylie, pointing. 'Goodness, this isn't the Garden of Eden, is it?'

'Well, we've plenty of snakes!' Kylie answered quite seriously.

'Have you ever seen a twenty-foot python, Miss Marshall?' Boyd Ballinger asked with a smile of warning.

'Don't let him rile you, Rosslyn, they're not here. *Are they?*' Kylie leaned over the seat and hit at her uncle's shoulder.

'Of course they are. Out in the rain forest and the swamps.'

'Oh, well then, we're not going there.'

'We will if you want to see a few crocs.'

Kylie shrieked. 'You're joking!' she said fervently.

47

'The greatest wish of my life is to see a *real* croc, not that silly stuffed thing in the gunroom!'

'That silly stuffed thing in the gunroom,' her uncle said patiently, 'almost cost your grandfather his life. This isn't the city, you know. Streets and buses and cars, a busy world of concrete. The crocodile has a perfect right up here, on the other hand a man on horseback has to cross a stream. That's what your grandfather had to do. He lost his horse, and later on a leg, but oddly enough he never lost his creepy fascination with crocodiles. When it goes right down to it they are pretty fantastic, hidden away in deep lagoons whose beauty would take your breath away. The natives count on some kind of spirit protection, and so help me, it works, but I'm pretty careful myself.'

'How horrible!' Rosslyn said, and shuddered, the colour whipping into her face, her golden eyes dilated, brilliant with just the thought of this vast uncharted tropical fantasy world. The sun slanted through the bauhinias and glinted off the tall, luxuriant grasses. Probably a snake lurked in that thick exotic carpet. She shivered again and Boyd Ballinger's laugh startled her.

'Don't worry, little one, I won't let anything happen to you!' The wind was tousling his thick black hair and there was a sardonic twist to his mouth. 'We look after our womenfolk up here.'

'Yes, actually he's a bit of a fusspot,' Kylie explained, her delphinium blue eyes everywhere. 'He's never offered to show me a croc before.'

'Well, that's one expedition I won't be going along

on!'

'Now that can't *be*, Rosslyn!' Boyd Ballinger caught her eyes in the mirror. 'Pretty nearly everyone who visits the Far North and the Territory is particularly anxious to see one.'

'I grant you, but for myself, I've no desire to make their acquaintance.'

'Well, we'll let that drop for a week or two,' he said casually. 'It's not of very great importance, and one must beat these little psychological hang-ups.'

'Don't worry, Rosslyn, I'm on *your* side, not on his. Uncle Boyd is the most dreadful tease. Still, think about it. I could never pass up that opportunity myself.'

'Naturally, you're a Ballinger!' her uncle pointed out.

'And I envy you to a degree,' Rosslyn smiled, determined not to be bothered by his attempts to bedevil her.

'Oh, look! Look right now!' Kylie began to bounce up and down on the seat. 'Belyando!' It was clear to all of them that Kylie considered she had come home. 'I love it!' she said softly, then again: 'I love it!'

Rosslyn's own expression changed. If they had been driving through a tropical fastness, here was civilization. A house like a snowy white egret, breasting the green hills. Sunlight splashed all over it, showing its rather unique irregularity that somehow managed to be extraordinarily satisfying. It followed no particular architectural style, unless it was for the deep Colonial verandahs that enclosed the main house on three sides.

Rather, it had grown along with the family and its fortunes, the verandah line broken into bays with each addition to the house. The original simple cottage, built by the first Anglo-Australian, Robert Douglas Ballinger, one of the State's earliest settlers, following a most distinguished military career, had been retained mostly for reasons of family sentiment, as the core of the main house, functioning in the present day as little more than part of the wide hallway that ran through to the rear of what was now a very large house.

The whole effect was quite splendid for what was basically a spacious Old Colonial home: the simple elegance of the white cast-iron panels that threw a delicate tracery of shade on to the polished diamond-shaped tiles of the sunlit verandah, the white wooden fretwork and the vine-wreathed pillars, the shiny greeny-black jalousied French doors that led out from each of the main rooms, the hipped roof with its deep protective slant painted in the same dark greeny-black of the shuttered doors.

The beautiful garden, though it had been very carefully laid out over fifty years before and since tended by an amount of labour, gave the strong impression that nature alone had decided on its arrangement, so brilliantly artless did it seem. It was riotously expressive of the tropics like some exotic painting of Gauguin's, full of showy colours and shapes, not the subtle muted colours and formal symmetry of the gardens Rosslyn was used to. This was nature in flamboyant abandon and on a grand scale, a fantastic and harmonious jumble of plants: the great clumps of decorative grasses, the pampas and the papyrus, the bamboo, the great banyan trees and glossy-leafed shrubs, tall spectacular lilies and vigorous-looking varieties of dahlias and zinnias and daisy-faced flowers of every conceivable colour, the great ivy-ribboned shade trees heavy with scarlet blossom, trailing the waxy bush orchids, the jasmine-tangled shade, and the glowing morning glories that decorated the glass-roofed white-latticed garden retreat set with white wrought-iron outdoor furniture with its plush daisy-patterned upholstery and hanging baskets of begonias and geraniums and the green and white spider plant that trailed from the rafters. Rosslyn's heart gave a small leap, for this was where she was going to live for the best part of eight weeks.

'You're going to be very happy here, Rosslyn,' Kylie said from the depths of her lonely little soul.

'I'm sure I am,' Rosslyn replied quietly, and pressed Kylie's hand. She felt mysteriously protected, though she was in reality in a very remote place. A brilliantly plumaged parrot perched on a twig screeched a loud welcome, and a fragrance like a tropical incense filled the air. Rosslyn took a deep breath, fully conscious now of her good fortune. This was adventure, and so far she had led a most uneventful life.

They swept up the broad driveway that circled a lily pond with a small fountain playing over a sculpture, which was one of Derek Ballinger's, was fashioned in bronze with enormous magenta rose lilies with purple mottled leaves clustered around its feet. It seemed to Rosslyn tremendously good, and she couldn't for the moment think too badly of Derek Ballinger. Perhaps true artists belonged to another world mute to the appeals of ordinary mortals. Perhaps it was a crazy idea for artists to get married in the first place and have children. It was every child's right to have love and attention, but evidently Derek Ballinger preferred to call in his stepbrother to stage-manage his life and his child.

A minute later they were all standing before this great tropical house with two dusky house girls appearing from nowhere and receiving instructions, responding with gentle voices when they were introduced to Rosslyn and keeping excessively merry smiles for Miz Ballinger and young Kylie. Surrounded by this all encompassing affection and approval, Kylie turned into a singularly happy-go-lucky child, bounding into the house and calling out:

'Ellie?'

'My governess when I was exactly six years old,' Boyd Ballinger explained. 'One of the best educated women in the State of Queensland for those days, an English lady of good family who practically reared me after my own mother died. We love Ellie. She's one of us, even when she's very much Eleanor as she is a lot of the time.'

'Couldn't she have supervised Kylie's studies, kept an eye on her?'

'No. Ellie's an old lady, you silly child. But don't tell *her* that. Besides, her life has been Belyando for the past thirty years. One could hardly expect her to keep abreast of modern teaching methods. I was sent off to a boarding-school myself when I was nine. Nine to seventeen. Four years at university. A trip around the world. Belyando, my life!'

Rosslyn could tell from his voice what it meant to him. And certainly he was the right man for his background – powerful, handsome, and extremely capable, not to say tough. There was a hardness about his lean body and firm jaw, a bud of green flame that burned brightly in his blue all-consuming glance. He was a man of vision and ambition and it affected everyone about him. Only *she* seemed the vaguely idiotic part of his plan. She would take good care not to faint on him again.

Her golden eyes, like Kylie's, looked feverishly excited.

'I want to thank you for inviting me to Belyando!' she said, exactly like a small girl at a party, and he smiled.

'You'll always be welcome in my home, Rosslyn, believe me. Ah, here's Ellie!' He took hold of Rosslyn's arm and led her up the four wide shallow stairs to the verandah, flanked by terra-cotta Ali Baba pots spilling out waves of a highly scented yellow gold flower. At the top of the stairs, hand outstretched, was a tall, very spare, silver-haired lady, with a severe, very distinguished face until she smiled, then the cool emphasis of her face broke up, and the remote formality turned into a look of irresistible warmth and intelligence.

'Welcome, my dear!' she said in an unmistakably English voice for all her long years in Australia. She had obviously formed Boyd Ballinger's baby drawl as well, for his own voice was quite cosmopolitan, even very convincingly cultivated. He began to introduce them and lazily suggested that Rosslyn might call the older lady 'Miss Eleanor' as Ellie's personality definitely did not invite informality in the early stages of acquaintance. Miss Eleanor dipped her silver head and thoroughly scrutinized Rosslyn without even appearing to do so. Then, apparently content, she led the way into the house with the sound of Kylie's voice singing some chant filling the air around them. Its indescribable happiness reminded Rosslyn vividly of her own childhood when she used to go to her grandparents' beautiful beach house for the holidays. If there was a solution for Kylie to be found, it would be here at Belyando.

CHAPTER THREE

SHE was happy. Every morning Rosslyn woke to the scent of strong coffee and freshly baked bread, the enormous quantities of scones that had to be ready for smoko, the crisp, fragrant breakfast rolls the men consumed with their T-bone steaks and fried eggs before the business of the day got under way. Each morning it was the same; the scents and the sounds, shafts of golden light splashing across her bed, glorious, matchless, light, an outbreak of birdsong, horses' hooves thudding, voices, distant calls, the orders, and the jokes and the muffled surprisingly mild curses, the white stockmen's voices, deep and drawly, the aboriginals' a merry sing-song, always on the verge of outright laughter. It fostered in Rosslyn a continuing sense of exhilaration and discovery.

The two weeks she had been on the property had flown. There was never a moment outside the daily two hours of tutorials that they could pin her to a chair. There was so much to be seen, so much to do. With some excellent, very patient, instruction from Boyd Ballinger and a good deal of practice walks, Rosslyn could manage her docile, sweet-mannered little mare Lucy quite well, but mostly she had a jeep at her disposal which even Kylie had to admit she managed a whole lot better. Whenever time offered, Boyd Ballinger took them on tours around the station, but there was so much of it, more than three thousand square miles, a great uncontrollable restlessness was upon Rosslyn to see as much as she could in the time that remained to her. Once the Big Wet set in, cattle work would come to a halt, so her time on the station was more than ordinarily busy. Each day mustering teams took off with their strings of work horses and loaded trailers, while the roping and branding, the feeding and breeding, the maintenance of property and the property boundary lines continued.

It seemed to Rosslyn from her travels around in the jeep that it would be a stupendous task. And dangerous. For although Belyando was alluringly beautiful, there were constant dangers in an environment that never ceased to resist man's efforts to conquer it. Not so many years before, sickness, accident, infection, snakebite could prove fatal; now Belyando, like the rest of the great stations of the vast Outback, could communicate with the rest of the country by way of its air power – in Belyando's case, three light aircraft and a helicopter that could carry men and equipment and set down virtually anywhere, and its two-way radio. However isolated a station, help was at hand in a very short time. The inevitable accidents went on, but the very toughness, the relentlessness of the environment seemed to breed a special kind of man.

With a big country and very few people to man it, loyalty to a family, to a station, was fierce. Most of the staff had been on Belyando all their lives and Belyando undertook to look after them, providing them with a good living and even entertaining them by means of a small movie theatre and an endless supply of popular recordings and classical, for Hart Ellis, the foreman, was oddly enough and opera buff, with the firm conviction that he had a good baritone voice himself, which he did not. There was not, however, a baritone role he could not attempt to sing in its original language and he was immune, or pretended to be, to all the good-natured ridicule and mock choruses that attended his many nocturnal performances. This was the way Rosslyn went to sleep, with the exotic perfume of jasmine and the night-blooming lilies, the Queen of the Night, and the sound of the great opera stars of the world, supported and accompanied by Hart Ellis, who was as thin and tough as a whiplash and a superb horseman. Hart's little aberrations, so far as the Boss was concerned, had to be condoned. He was too valuable to be asked more than to 'tone it down'.

So it was a two-way affair, then, the business of living in a remote spot, the unhesitating co-operation, the respect, even deep affection, that every man, woman and child on the station seemed to have for the Boss. Boyd to nearly all of them he might be, but he was very much, for all his democratic ways, a kind of benevolent overlord, responsible for this vast remote settlement and the large-scale financial investment of the entire Ballinger family scattered over three States. The head of each family unit was a shareholder in a venture that demanded very considerable financial resources, in recent years, the large-scale clearing of the rain jungle and the aerial sowing of new pastures.

Once a year, over the August holidays when the

South was still shivering and the tropics basked in superlative weather, there was an annual meeting of Ballinger shareholders, the entire family business assembly, conducted very formally along the most exacting board meeting rules, with the fun held until later when all matters pertaining to the station were discussed and put to the vote for settlement. Boyd Ballinger, as major shareholder and Chairman, a kind of family hero figure, who presided over their fortunes, hosted and attended all these, and Belyando was filled to capacity with relatives and children. Even eight-year-old Kylie would in time come into her Belyando shares, as she was the first to tell one.

Belyando was a cattle empire, a true success story, but it had claimed a few lives, including that of Deborah Ballinger, Boyd's mother, who had neglected what she thought of as a mere scratch, suffered blood poisoning and died before she was thirty years old. In consequence, all injuries on the station, however minor, had to be reported, and each one of them received tetanus shots and boosters.

In spite of this, none of them wished to leave or enjoy what the big cities had to offer. The annual cramming at vacation time proved more than enough. What attracted them all was challenge, man's constant desire to conquer his environment. What held them was the overwhelming sense of space and freedom, the feeling of being at one with the earth and the sky, the birds and the animals. Nature as close and familiar as a mother's face, allowing a man to grow and know himself.

Even Rosslyn had the feeling that she was no longer the girl she had been only a few short weeks ago. She seemed to be blossoming like the clusters of moonlight cactus that released their heavy perfume each night beneath her window. Each day the sun wheeled across the sky in barbaric splendour, each night the stars came out so big and brilliant, it seemed she had never seen stars before, the blazing trail of the Milky Way where legend said dwelt the souls of the departed, the Southern Cross, like a dazzling colour-fluctuating kite set aloft by the trade winds. There was even a degree of desperation in the way Rosslyn was enjoying herself, as though it could all be snatched away from her at a moment's notice.

Boyd Ballinger, catching sight of her small, rapt face, often smiled to himself, remembering the cool, polite little way she had accepted his invitation. She was very slight, very graceful, very decorative indeed and she had proved of immense value with Kylie. He was content. Even Ellie couldn't fault the girl, but rather thought up all sorts of adventures to fill each waking moment. So it was a time of discovery for Rosslyn, all the more intense, for soon the monsoon would wheel across the land bringing perhaps a cyclone. One never knew.

That morning, dressed in cotton slacks and a bright sunflower cotton knit halter, Rosslyn joined Kylie down at the corrals where Kylie was having a splendid time watching Hart Ellis break in the wild bush horses. Hart, dust-covered and laconic, seemed to be having more difficulty controlling his colourful language in front of the girls than dealing with the high-mettled brumbies. Yet the work was tough and very dangerous with the enraged horses dancing on their hind legs, bucking and kicking, doing mad frightened circuits of the breaking yards. None of this string had ever known bridle or saddle and the mad spirit of independence was there in their frothing mouths and white-ringed eyes. Quite a few of the other stockmen and the aboriginal boys lined the fence shouting encouragement to Hart and a few insults mixed up with endearments to the big bay straight in from the bush.

It was a fine-looking animal, muscles heaving, coat glistening, standing trembling and ready to explode while Jacky-O, Hart's aboriginal offsider, threw a saddle cloth over the colt's back, with the hind leg nearest him secured by a rope to avoid a certain uninhibited swipe.

'The horse can't kick now!' Kylie explained authoritatively, her enthralled little face half hidden by a blue silk bandana, a smudge of red dust across the bridge of her nose and under one eye like a trail of ritual ochre.

'It doesn't look like that to me!' Rosslyn replied, edging them both back a little, though they were sitting on the white fence of an adjacent corral and not enjoying the full benefit of the curling dust castles thrown up by the bay's churning hooves. The stockmen appeared oblivious to them, whistling and offering cautious advice. It was Boyd Ballinger who had decreed where they were to sit and he had had the devil's own job getting Kylie to agree until he suggested she might not want to attend at all.

Hart was busy telling the bay they were 'mates, you beauty! I won't hurt you!' in a voice Rosslyn reserved for babies, then Hart spoilt the whole thing by biting off a picturesque curse as the bay decided to rear madly in protest. In the yard beyond, the bay's real mates, the other brumbies, snorted and cavorted in open sympathy with their oppressed bush companion.

'This looks terribly dangerous to me,' Rosslyn breathed, watching Hart's attempt to tie the straps under the colt's trembling belly.

'Oh, don't worry!' Kylie said, soothing her. 'Hart is one of the best. Uncle Boyd is the best, but Mummy says he has no business going around trying to break his neck. He's too valuable. If you think Hart's strong, you should see Uncle Boyd!' Without warning, Kylie suddenly slapped the fence and directed a powerful, ear-splitting shriek towards Hart, who for once appeared to have met his match. A furious, dislodging buck had sent him sprawling to the ground, and, infamy of infamies, his best ten-gallon hat was battered and kicked shapeless under the bay's vicious hooves. Fire flashed in its eyes, then it made a triumphant circuit of the corral, passing very deliberately near the fence and sending the catcalling aboriginal boys flying for cover.

'That must have hurt,' Kylie observed ruefully.

'I can believe it. Anyone else who trys to ride that brumby might join him!'

'That was a powerful fall, all right!' Kylie swung around brightly. 'Oh, heavens, we're in for a miracle! Uncle Boyd is going to ride him.'

'Children!' Boyd Ballinger acknowledged them lightly, coming up behind them, a tall, very tantalizing presence at Rosslyn's shoulder. 'Enjoying yourselves?'

'We're doing our level best!' Rosslyn informed him. 'It's Mr. Ellis who's not faring so well.'

'Hart doesn't need any sympathy,' he said, eyeing her lazily, 'he's been breaking horses since he was a boy. The big bay will make a good work horse for the next muster, don't you worry!'

'Listen . . .' Kylie said, as though struck by a great idea. 'Ride him for us, will you?'

'If it will amuse you?'

'Please don't do it for me,' begged Rosslyn, peering rather fearfully at him. 'It looks awfully dangerous!'

'I'll take my hat off,' he said, condescending. 'Hart, you may retire from the field.'

'That's very generous of you, Boss. He's a hard 'un. Strong, good legs, plenty of spirit.'

'It's only to amuse the children.'

'Right-oh!' Hart jerked his head round. 'Here, chuck a bag over the nag's head, you ass. Quiet him, a bit. 'Struth, Jacky, you're sillier than I gave you credit for. Get 'im over by the rails, the Boss will mount him there.'

Jacky-O's chocolate-coloured skin appeared livid, but he inched near the wild bay.

'Oh, this is marvellous, isn't it?' Kylie moaned.

'I don't really know. It must be dreadful for the horse!'

'Well, I never!' said Kylie, looking very tolerantly

exasperated, a fair imitation of her uncle. '*I* have to go to school, don't *I*? I don't want to. The same with the horse. He has to be schooled too. He'll have a lot of work to do. He has to be disciplined. This is a big station and we need plenty of horses. So there's no use his fighting it. Uncle Boyd will ride him, you'll see!'

And ride him he did! A hard fight all the way, but there was never the moment when the man wasn't in command, as though he had been born into this tropical wilderness expressly to tame horses. Like Hart, he was a superb horseman, but more elegant, more fluid in his movements, unless it was his own physical perfection, riding upright in the saddle now, his dark face caked with dust, the radiant sun savage enough to make him screw up his eyes to mere slits, the tiring colt moving away from the wild rearing and bucking, its sides sweating and heaving, until gradually it checked, then began walking sedately around the perimeter of the corral. It had all come to an end with dramatic swiftness and Rosslyn found she could take a breath. Her eyes were glowing feverishly, very largely born of speculations on disaster and an unwilling excitement. The sight of man and horse held her as if she was spellbound.

The big bay had given up after its brief, helpless struggle. It stood quietly, received a few pats on the rump, some encouraging words, then Boyd Ballinger dismounted, a mere nothing in his point of view, but something quite remarkable to Rosslyn, who had a certain defensiveness about her own lack of skill. He had been reared in the bush. This was his life. This was the way of it. Even so she knew she was looking at a master horseman, his bronze polished features made more prominent by the fine shading of red dust. His eyes glittered like green fire, all the blue washed out of them, and she couldn't drag her glance from him.

Kylie was lavish with her praise. 'You little beauty!' she raved. 'That was terrific, Uncle Boyd. The day has been saved!'

'That was very brave!' Rosslyn seconded, thinking he must surely hear the fast bird flutter of her heart.

'Don't be silly!'

'Cruel too,' she added, because she couldn't help herself and would be forever on the side of the loser.

'Yes, it is in a way!' he murmured, studying her. 'The taste for freedom burns brightly in all of us. I know horses as well as any man. Pretty soon that bay is going to develop into a good work horse, and that's what we need. Out here, a man's horse is his friend, his only companion for weeks at a stretch. Our horses are treated well. That one will survive.'

'I know,' she said, bending to his will. 'It's just the discipline, I suppose. No one likes it.'

'You included. Didn't I tell you to wear a hat?'

'Won't this scarf do as well?'

'No, it won't!' he said emphatically, and lifted it clear of her head so that her hair emerged flamelike, dancing curls in the sunlight. His well defined mouth moved in a smile, his expression rather hard and provoking. 'Want to come up in the chopper? I have to drive a hundred or so head out of the thick scrub. The men have a portable pen rigged up.'

Kylie began to hop up and down. 'What about me?'

'You have plenty of good times!' her uncle said. 'Well, Rosslyn, are you chicken?'

'Why don't you say *again*? That's what you mean.'

'Don't exaggerate, little one. I mean no such thing!'

'Well, naturally I'm interested,' she said, tossing her head, 'however, without doing it on purpose, I'm allergic to light aircraft!'

'I'll grant you that, and there must be some motivation?'

'No. It's purely physical, I assure you. No psychological hang-ups whatever. I've flown many times in a jet. On the whole, they're a big improvement.'

His blue-green eyes were brilliantly sardonic. 'Rosslyn, if you're going to spend any time on Belyando, you'll have to get used to something a whole lot smaller. A jet wouldn't be much use to me out here. Now, quite early in the peace might be the best idea for you, and naturally I'll proceed with extreme caution. Can't you feel I want to keep you happy?'

Despite herself, excitement prickled her veins. It would be absurdly easy to ... Hastily she thrust away that idea, but it lingered, *and* the danger, for he appeared to be a mind-reader. 'The suspicion has crossed my mind!' was all she would volunteer. 'Thank you, Mr. Ballinger, I should like to come up with you.'

Kylie suddenly seized the opportunity to speak while

the grown-ups were duelling with their eyes. 'A lot of things aren't right round here!' she announced. 'Rosslyn is *my* friend. Can't I come?'

'No!' her uncle said firmly.

'All right!' Kylie was surprisingly without resentment. 'It just so happens Ellie and I are going to do some great posters for Christmas. You know the sort of thing.'

'Santa Claus, reindeers?' her uncle teased her.

'Sure. I've heard of those things. No, it just so happens I've got a better idea!'

'You have?' Rosslyn's golden glance whipped around, thoroughly diverted from Boyd Ballinger's tall, lean figure.

'Yes, and I'm not letting on until Christmas, so there!'

'Really? How interesting!'

'You're a sweet, adorable child!' her uncle said with a quick smile, 'and I'm looking forward to seeing the results of your magnificent project. But for now, let's get back to the house. I'm literally tasting the dust. We'll take off some time after lunch, Rosslyn. You'll get an aerial view of the back country and it might even turn out a pleasure trip, who knows?'

'Lucky devil!' Kylie muttered, starting to sag.

'I thought you made it clear you were looking forward to a most interesting afternoon with Ellie?' her uncle commented, looking down at her glossy head.

'So I am,' Kylie maintained with no zest at all. 'What *we'll* have is a very good time.'

'Well then?' He flicked at her curls, rousing her out of

66

it. 'How is it you get prettier every day?' he asked.

Kylie stood stock still under his hand, her blue eyes sparkling with a deep satisfaction as if he had presented her with the most enchanting gift. 'If you weren't my uncle, I'd want to marry you when I grow up.'

'My darling,' he said without laughing, 'when you grow up you're going to be a tremendous success. A positive personality.'

'You're not serious?'

'I am. You'll see. In the meantime let's get back to the house and you can get going on those posters.'

'I'll never show them to Daddy,' Kylie said, with a quick look at Rosslyn. 'He'd burn them!'

'He's a trifle tactless, I grant you, but let's say, poppet, this time he'll have to go around me. It just so happens I remember your father's early struggles. There was a time he was as uncertain of himself as you are now.'

'Now he's doing beautifully. *Too* well!' Kylie said with unchildlike violence. 'I wish he was still struggling, then he would have time for me!'

'I never said he struggled exactly,' her uncle pointed out. 'Derek has always been used to many fine meals and a very stylish establishment. Still, things weren't easy for him. The first time your grandfather Ballinger heard Derek wanted to be a professional artist he nearly died laughing, then, less hurtful, threatened to cut him out of his will. Your father's earliest efforts weren't taken all that seriously and Derek grew thinner and thinner and more deadly in earnest and more difficult, and in the end he had to move to the city,

67

where he met your mother. I must say your mother has never laughed at his ability. In fact I've heard her say many times that she was the only one to recognize Derek's great gift and promote his success. She must have forgotten your grandmother Richards called him "the boy wonder" for years and the Ballinger family council set him up in business. There's any amount of evidence of that, and I like to stick as far as possible to the facts.'

'Yes, incredible, isn't it?' Kylie said with a philosophic shrug, another fair imitation of her uncle. 'I'm so glad I'm a Ballinger!'

'It has its advantages!' her uncle agreed lightly, then suddenly swooping, he picked her up and hoisted her on to his shoulder.

Kylie laughed and enthused. Life was glorious! and it was going to be terribly simple. Uncle Boyd, with his genius for timing, had assured her that what gifts she had would never be wasted, and right at that moment Kylie started to grow up.

Twenty miles out they caught sight of the missing herd.

'Look down there!'

Rosslyn obeyed the terse command. At first she could see nothing in the eerie bush, then her eyes began to make out the dark shapes of the sheltering cattle, thickly clustered in the long grass and around the base of the trees. They were boxed up, about a hundred of them, in a fairly inaccessible hide, country that had to be feared and respected. All along they had been making careful sweeps of the likely places, the water-holes and the thick grasslands, and here was the herd in much the spot Boyd Ballinger expected.

Rosslyn sat absolutely still, almost frozen into immobility, looking through the canopy out over the coning blade of the rotor. The helicopter banked, then straightened, then went down in a slow vertical dive, skimming the trees. The cattle looked up rather dreamily at the invader, then as though charged by an electric current they sprang off in a body, galloping wildly out of the scrub.

I can master my fears. I can. *I can!* Rosslyn crossed both arms rigidly around herself. It would take a lot of practice, but she could do it. This kingdom of Belyando was stripping away every layer of her civilized skin. She was learning to live with danger. The helicopter dropped down over the trees, the whirring flow of the rotor sending the cattle charging, heads down, in a kind of blind desperation to get away from it, bulls, bullocks in the lead, heifers and cows, all of the animals full grown, an arrowhead formation of jostling, bellowing bodies, thundering the earth in a weirdly disciplined-looking stampede, violently pounding up the lush grasses and the swirling sea of yellow and red wild flowers, sweating and frantic with fear.

The helicopter whirred above them, driving them on, banking and flanking, gathering them in this way and that. It was an extraordinarily effective feat of mustering from the air. A good mile away, in a relatively clear patch of ground, several stockmen had set up a portable enclosure, part of the endless cattle routine. They were mounted now, stockwhips at the ready, anticipating the moment when the first wave of cattle would pound towards them like a fast moving current. The helicopter pinpointed their flight, so the stockmen waited, vastly alert, catching sight now of the lead bullocks as they broke cover, with the tormenting air machine whirring on ahead.

'Hy yaah! ha yaah!' Voices threw up on the wind. Whips crackled and lashed, beating above the roar of the cattle. One moment it was certain to be a deafening débâcle, then almost as if someone had trod on a powerful brake, the leaders slowed up like magic, their furious bellowing rush petering out to near nothing. The rest of the herd followed them right into the enclosure, a few strays surging out and quickly gathered in with a flick on the rump. Slouch hats made wide circles in the air, the signal for the successful completion of the mission, and a piece of aerial mustering of the first rank.

Boyd Ballinger held his hand up, palm outstretched, they hovered a minute more over the area, then they banked away to the left. Away to the pandanus thickets and the tea-tree swamps that beckoned from the air.

'Well now, young Rosslyn,' his brilliant eyes slid over her with emphasis, 'that was a pretty severe test. I thought you came through rather well.'

'Astonishing, but I think life out here, close to danger, might make one less afraid, don't you think?'

He looked a trifle surprised, his flaring black brows came together. 'Perhaps. A few other things are neces-

70

sary – courage, endurance, stamina. You can imagine the hardships and setbacks the pioneers suffered. This country can be savagely beautiful, but it's fairly inhospitable to man as the conqueror. It's a world teeming with wild life, and it's very fascinating, even when some enormous, waddling thing comes right at you out of a swamp. The forty miles of the Gulf swarm with crocs, the rivers of the Cape, though they've shot plenty out.'

Rosslyn looked back at him, fastening a bright curl behind her ear. 'Well, I wouldn't have missed that aerial muster for anything. I'm a misfit out here, I know. I'm sure I'd make a terrible hand at station life.'

'And I'm determined that's not going to be the case!'

'Whatever do you mean?'

He was not looking at her but straight ahead and he didn't even bother replying. Only his amused little laugh reached her. She hesitated, her golden eyes glowing, then wisely started out on another track.

'Strangely enough I feel safer in this chopper than I did in the Aztec!'

'Cherokee Six!' he corrected her, his voice very lazy and taunting. 'The Aztec is the *other* one, the one with the yellow and black stripes. The Aztec is our work horse. It can carry loads of up to a ton and fuel for a thousand miles, and it can operate off the shortest roughest fields. We've got a good all-weather strip here, and it cost plenty, but you should see some of the places I've landed. Now what about seeing some of the bird life?'

Without even waiting for an answer they whirred off towards the lagoon, festooned with waving reeds and blue waterlilies in great expanses on the glittering, dark green surface. Ducks and black swans were floating across it and jabirus, tall as a man, and snowy white egrets stalked the shallows, swallowing down the tender green shoots from the waterlilies.

'Can we put down?' Rosslyn leaned forward, peering, completely giving herself up to the exotica of the moment.

'Are you sure you want to?'

'If you've the time, of course!'

'Time has nothing to do with it.'

She met his jewel-coloured eyes and just for a moment it wasn't the thought of the flowering wilderness that was engulfing her.

'Why not?' she asked, blinking, trying to break his spell. 'I'm going to see all the best of Belyando while I'm here.'

'Yes. Just like a sweet little girl removed very briefly from your own world. All right, young Rosslyn, if it's adventure you want . . . I'm all for it, myself!'

The exact tone of his voice was downright perturbing, rather hard and amused at once. 'Well, I can't be involved in anything *too* dangerous,' she said. 'And forget all those twenty-foot pythons and other rip-roaring stuff.'

'No *story*!' he put her suggestion firmly aside. 'I've seen a few in the rain jungle. Claw marks in runways. But I'll tell you what I'll do. I won't let anything take you by surprise. Everywhere you look there'll be something. Just keep hold of my arm. If the worst comes to the worst, I can pick you up and make a run for it. The only trouble is you're so small I have a feeling I might crush you.'

'And *I've* a feeling you're trying to frighten me!'

'Surely not! Why, my darling girl, you're going to step out into a tropical wilderness, not a beach party. The jungle can make a fascinating study if you look at it in the right light. There'll be plenty of snakes about, but most of them harmless. A goanna or two, some over six feet. For someone like you they'll probably be invisible, unless you step on one by mistake and they start hissing. Horrible!'

His eyes were moving lightly over her creamy gold, vulnerable face. 'Still coming?'

'Yes. I can't resist it. Besides, it seems a long time since I had the earth under my feet.'

'Right!' His eyes searched out a likely landing place with deadly accuracy. They came down in a whirling bubble of heat, the skids sinking then standing firmly on the thick grass. Her choice had been made, now she had no other alternative but to go ahead and meet the blossom-filled air, and the excited chatter of the lustrous parrots that were as intent on her as she was on them.

The sun fell over her beautiful skin and her hair, dazzling her eyes so that she averted her head to show the lovely sweep of her throat and chin. Boyd Ballinger seemed completely unconcerned by the sight of this very young Eve in a wild Eden stopping negligently to select a yellow-gold wild flower to push through her hair.

'There! A little local colour. Now you're absolutely perfect!'

She went to say something, but her voice shook and died in her throat. His eyes were startlingly vivid and it was folly to look into them, but physical attraction, as she was finding, was a powerful thing, unreasoning, blotting out any sense of caution.

'I've never been able to resist a redhead!' he said, smiling at her rather entranced stare.

'What a self-opinionated man!'

'God forbid. I'm sure of myself, Rosslyn, which is a different thing! The dark bronze of his skin emphasized the shockingly bright colour of his eyes, blue-green-golden flecks, the jet black hair with its deep crisp wave. Knowledge of her own weakness began to fill her with a passionate resentment, a desire not to capitulate to his undoubted attraction. His expression was very hard and disconcerting, very intent in quality for all the smile on his curving mouth. She had the strangest feeling that somewhere, even in a dream, this had all happened before.

'So you're clairvoyant too?' he asked very oddly.

'I simply don't know . . .'

'Oh, stop!' he said rather curtly. 'This is inevitable. The battle of the sexes and you're winning hands down. That makes me a bit angry. Come on, let's go look at the lagoon. I refuse to commit myself beyond that.'

He moved very swiftly and Rosslyn had to hurry to

catch up with him.

'Are you running away?'

'It seems like it. There's a limit to the amount of provocation I can take.'

A thousand sensations seemed to whirl up and hit her and she clutched at his arm. His own hands moved very swift and purposeful, holding her fast just above the elbows, an aura of crisis about his jet black head. 'Let's look at you.'

'What are you trying to do?'

'Absolutely nothing. Hold your face up. I *can* look at you, can't I? Russet, and rose and gold, the soft glitter of your hair. You look exactly how I like a woman to look.'

'I don't believe it,' she said in an acute state of tension. 'I'm sure I don't bear the least resemblance to your ideal woman.'

'Very beautiful and endearing at once,' he said as though he hadn't heard her. 'The two don't always go together.'

A huge velvety butterfly drifted by with a series of orange circles on its wingtips, a silent witness.

'In fact, Rosslyn, it would be very easy to fall in love with you. All the cards neatly stacked in your favour. God knows where I'm finding the strength to resist you, but resist you I must. Doe eyes reproaching me.'

'How exactly like a man! I'm not reproaching you at all.'

'Well, what *are* you doing? A woman's eyes always tell when she's ready to be made love to or not.'

A feverish singing started up in her blood. 'Oh, I

don't think I have to endure this,' she said a little wildly. 'There's too big a gap between us.'

'*Yes!*' he said without the slightest preamble. 'And all sorts of complications. *So . . .* we'll concentrate on the wild life. That's what we're here for. So *you* said.'

'What's more, I meant it! I may seem like a rank amateur to you, Mr. Ballinger, but I assure you I've no designs on you.'

'And *I* think you have!' he drawled outrageously, his opal-coloured eyes glimmering between their thick webbing of lashes. 'Without trying, if you like. What's the difference? You're giving me a bad case of the jitters and I'm anxious to preserve my bachelor standing!'

'And I'm not inviting you to change it!'

'You're saying one thing, Rosslyn, but you're looking quite another! You're not going to mark me up as one of your trophies!'

'What you actually mean is you're attracted to me?'
'Yes.'

'How unforeseen!' she said sarcastically.

'Not exactly. You looked like that to me from the beginning.'

'Well, that upsets your little scheme.'

'I haven't got one.'

'And you think *I* have?'

'I know essentially, you're some kind of enchantress. Maybe you're still serving your apprenticeship, but you're an enchantress all right. Probably I'd get used to you in time. Right now, it's only my demonic will that's keeping me playing it mighty cool!'

She drew a long quivering breath and her eyelashes fell. What could she say? So she stood there utterly defenceless and not caring in the least what he did. So far as she was concerned, he was unique, a kind of private dream she told no one about, including herself. His hand shot out and clamped around her wrist with a wholly male strength and impatience.

'Come along, little one,' he said without a great deal of self-conviction. 'Be guided by someone a whole lot older and wiser. This might look like some kind of romantic idyll, but you're up against severe self-discipline – on my part. I know *you* don't care if I kiss you senseless, but I'm determined to stand on the side-lines. Quite apart from any other consideration, I just happen to care about you. You're a very sweet little girl and I must follow the rules. I was brought up a gentle-man and I'm going to stick with it if it kills me. So we'll go for an educational excursion down to the lagoon, feed the ducks if you like, then I'll take you back home. Routine. What did I tell you, you're just another Kylie.'

She tried to smile, but it looked faintly desperate, almond eyes glowing, the wind blowing through her short curls, and cooling her flushed cheeks. 'Please don't say any more. You're upsetting me.'

'I'm sorry. It's not your fault anyway. The truth is you provoke me beyond measure. Put it down to the tropics. Seduction in the sun and all the rest of it. Can't you understand that?'

'It's not intentional!' she almost whispered, knowing

that wasn't the truth either.

'Is that supposed to make it any better?' he asked dryly.

Her delicate shoulder withdrew from under his hand, though every nerve in her body was imploring that same hand to tighten. This frightening, stormy longing had to pass. She moved quickly away from him across the grassy savannah, thick and soft under her feet. The very sight of him hurt her senses when his voice alone would have made her fall in love with him. Young and foolish, the perfect description. She was out of her depth in a strange new world. But such a beautiful world! Tiny birds flitted to and fro, bright red and yellow, the plump little honey-eaters, turquoise blue on the back, and purple and green on the breast feathers, like the enamelling on jewellery. Just ahead, like quicksilver in the sunlight, shimmered the moon-shaped lagoon. It was fringed, almost walled in by bush willows and tea-tree, casuarinas and spiky pandanus that grew out over the water at an odd angle.

The air on the savannah was very fresh and clean, yet as they grew nearer the lagoon it became heavy with some kind of ghostly perfume, like a musky incense, the startlingly beautiful alabaster lilies that showed their luminous faces above the pale green shoots of the reeds. A greeny-grey snake, the same colour as the jungle, slithered apprehensively away from her foot, but Rosslyn didn't notice it, as she stared ahead at the lagoon. Through the tracery of trees she could see a whole colony of silver grey cranes with rufous-coloured heads gathering their food. The sight was so beautiful and so rare to her it seemed almost unbelievable, like a picture book or a dream. These were the dancing brolgas, that could bob and bow and form a quadrille, and they were almost as fascinating just stalking the reed flats or throwing up blue lotus flowers and gobbling the long juicy stalks.

They came to a halt in the shadows, a peculiar ring of greeny gold light. Even in this remote secret spot bougainvillea, like a tongue of flame, made a frenzied sweep down a great paperbark and landed almost at Rosslyn's feet. The magic of the moment moved in her and she felt as though she truly stood within a charmed circle. Iridescent water-flies flickered before her eyes. There were ferns in myriads, from a delicate type of maidenhair to luxuriant tree-like growth. The wind had dropped and there was only the sound of the birds and the rustling of leaves. The thick lily pads floated on a sea of melted green glass that threw up complete reflections of the wading birds and the leafy arms of the trees. As a scene it was ravishing to the senses, even to the ferocious-looking bearded lizard that was sunning itself on a big moss-covered rock.

'What a wonderful sight!' she whispered.

'Everything looks beautiful because you're young and sensitive to such things. Could you live with it? The heat and the wet and a cyclone or two. This all looks like a dream, but there's reality too!'

'I know that. I'm learning. You're too hard on me.'

'Perhaps. Look over there!' Boyd's tone was very casual and she was unprepared for the sight of a fallen log rear up and lash its tail like a monster. She could feel herself trembling and she slammed back right into him in instinctive recoil. The gigantic lizard, its basking disturbed, stood erect now, its forked purple tongue whipping belligerently in and out of its gaping jaws. This was the monitor, famous for its ability to search out the nests of crocodiles and gorge itself on the eggs. It stood its ground, hissing and slashing, a good five feet from nose to tail with chainmail armour and vicious talons.

'Oh!' she said, shuddering.

'*Oh?* I thought you just said you were learning!'

'So I am, but I'd like to take my time with those monsters.'

'A goanna!' he corrected her. 'A big one, admittedly, but we're in no danger at all. I mean it. So stop trembling!'

'We all react differently.'

'We sure do!'

'Well I dare say if *I* saw a goanna every time I went for a stroll, I'd be used to it too. Could we move on now, do you think?'

'Don't you want to see it run?' he mocked her. 'It's quite something – shinning up the nearest tree, clawing off the bark!'

'I believe you. I'll just get behind you, if you don't mind, and clutch at your sleeve. I'm not out for trouble.'

'Why not?' he asked her, swinging her behind him. 'Adventure is the spice of life!'

'That's cheering, but I'm not used to it either!'

'Why, Rosslyn, with just a little encouragement I'm sure you'd come along very quickly. Never forget you're – *spunky,* wasn't it?'

'Oh, here we go again!' she moaned. 'There've been plenty of times I wanted to say something about you and I haven't!'

'You meant to say you wanted to and you didn't?'

'I'll never score off you. Don't ask me why.'

'It wouldn't do you any good if you did! Now, just to answer our problem, there goes our friend!'

The goanna, its reptilian head looking very vengeful and suspicious, suddenly turned away from them with complete indifference and began a surprisingly swift and ungainly run down to the lagoon, slithered madly into the water and swam away.

'Better now?' His mocking glance touched her face.

'Much better, thank you.'

'No, don't take your hand away. I rather like that soft clutch at my sleeve. Besides, I won't tell anyone you were frightened.'

Belatedly Rosslyn let go of his arm and gave a wry little smile. 'What you must think of me!'

'Do you really want to know?' There was a decided edge to his voice and his eyes glittered green.

For a shaken, shocked moment she didn't care what she said. 'Tell me, who's to hear or know?' she said recklessly. She swung her arms above her head in a graceful, abandoned gesture, feeling the quick surge of adrenalin that ran through her slender body. The sun flared over her rose-amber head, struck pale gold from the creamy surface of her skin. She looked very lovely and slightly unpredictable, her golden eyes very large and brilliant, an odd mixture of pleading and a rather frantic invitation. There was simply too much excitement to him and it hammered away at her until it began to draw a dangerous, irresistible response. The truth was she was filled with a sensual awareness of him that made her undergo a curious transformation, when she turned from a delicate and graceful young girl, rather reticent in her fashion, into Eve herself, fully aware of her own beauty and power. For the first time in her life she was using this power deliberately, knowing what he could do and unwilling to stop herself. There was enchantment here. There *had* to be, when she could still feel secure in a dangerous element. She only knew with complete certainty that he meant a great deal to her – the charm and the humour and the hard little patches that made her quiver.

Boyd's mouth now was twisted in a kind of amused exasperation as though she was Kylie in the middle of a drama, but his eyes were something else again – a pure shock of colour, very alert and sharply sardonic. Rosslyn was just that bit afraid of those eyes. They were intensely male for all their jewelled sparkle and damnably sure of themselves. It was this complete self-assurance that gave her pause.

'Having second thoughts, I hope?' he asked dryly.

'About what?'

'About fascinating me,' he said in a hard, mocking voice. 'You're giving a very striking display at the moment.'

'Oh, that's cruel!'

'It's the truth.'

'Then why are you afraid?'

'*Afraid?*' That apparently was a word he didn't admit into his vocabulary. His smile hardened and his eyes leapt into brilliant life, turbulent even, his height and his dark, vivid masculinity a sudden menace. 'Now *that*, flower face, was very foolish, and you can't throw the question away. We have to do something about it and I have a feeling it will be pretty soon!'

'All right, you're not afraid!' she said, shivering, drowning in the long grass, under the strange pull of the lily-covered lagoon. Perhaps a debil-debil lived there, putting a spell on her. There was no one like Boyd Ballinger and there never would be again, not for her. She was a victim of her own intense femininity, however innocently dormant up until then. Here was shattering excitement and she was letting it sweep her along, the colour racing up under her skin, putting her heart and her mind in two different places. Her heart was here in this dreamlike fantasy jungle full of birds and billabongs and gorgeous lotus flowers. Her sound common sense that she had prided herself on was a thousand miles away at Morlands.

The air was electric between them like the moments before a thunderstorm and Boyd was speaking in an undertone when there were only the water birds and the bush creatures to hear them. Through the lacy green willows she could see the snowy white egrets courting and nesting. The wind too had dropped and there was only the sound of rustling in the undergrowth and the soft swish of the little flowers of the sunrise that grew all around her and she was disturbing with the agitated and unconscious movement of her hand.

He walked towards her and she could no more have resisted him than the wild flowers could have resisted the sun and the rain. His hands closed over her shoulders, swift and purposeful, as though he was giving in to a spur of the moment necessity to shake her, and even if he was hurting her there was an intense, bittersweet pleasure in it.

'Not a very good idea to provoke me, Rosslyn. You're not all grown up yet.'

'I will be one day.'

'Really? Why not today? Stop talking, this is all I care about. Kissing a rose. Satiny skin, silky mouth!'

He was talking under his breath and she felt the muscles of his hand and arm tighten. The unleashed sensuality of his expression was dazzling her, a manifestation of a treacherous, unguarded attraction he had no real wish for. She closed her eyes at the quick clamour of her own senses and he took her fully into his arms, thrusting his hand through her bright hair, holding her head back tightly, as if she wished to escape from him. She could feel herself trembling, but she offered no resistance, just gave herself up to his overwhelming questing urgency.

His lips touched her throat first, lingered on the pulse, then as though they could no longer resist her, moved to her mouth. Her breath caught and she twisted slightly in his arms, and he relented his hold a little without moving his mouth, then brought her back into the hard circle of his arms so that she knew quite well she was no bird that could fly out of reach.

All the limits of her experience were instantly set aside. There seemed no sensation he could not draw from her, and no use pretending he couldn't. She was enormously dependent on him, though it was clear that the rare woman, if anyone, had given him so much pleasure. He wanted to kiss her, she knew that. A few moments when he was defeated by her acute femininity, a desirability that was very real, and kiss her he did, with such mastery and intense passion it dispelled every single difference and consideration between them. No evasion was possible. A mutual sensuous current linked them with growing warmth and power.

It was breathtaking. It was frightening. A radiant entity with a will and life of its own. For a brief second, Rosslyn grasped at the fact that there are forces beyond one's control. She accepted it as something inexorable, against which she had no defence, not even if she possessed all the wisdom of the world. She had lost her breath and presently she would lose all sense of herself. But what did it matter, when everything was perfect? There was always the captive who never wished to be set free. Always a woman, and she felt so much like a woman it didn't seem possible she could turn into a girl again. Boyd had shown her her own passionate nature so that she melted into his dominating embrace with the whole world spinning away from them and she absurdly uncaring.

When he thrust her away from him with a kind of soft violence, it felt like an actual betrayal. A fierce but short-lived loving ... now this? She felt dizzy and disorientated, her skin paled to ivory, her mouth throbbing, and he reached out and held her still as if she was in danger of falling.

'You're a miracle, Rosslyn.'

She saw his eyes and she could still say sadly: 'But you want me to go.'

'Even Belyando isn't going to be big enough for both of us after this.'

'Well, don't expect *me* to see the humour of it!'

'You will!' His turquoise-green glance held her a prisoner. 'And don't look back at me as if I've a very grievous sin on my conscience. You're over twenty-one.'

'Yes, I know! I suppose that was inevitable, but I'd much rather it hadn't happened.'

'Try to accept it gracefully, flower face. No sense in resenting your own weakness.'

He looked so bold and careless with the sun gilding his high cheekbones she felt spirit thrill through her veins. 'Let's get a few basic facts right, Mr. Ballinger. *You* were kissing me!'

'I know!' His laughter was low and laconic. 'It's costing me an effort not to kiss you again, but all my old jungle training is returning. Let's shake hands instead and agree to forget it. Anyone can make a mistake. The great thing is not to do it again!'

'Right, it's a deal! I'd do anything for you, Mr. Ballinger.' Her voice came out very soft and husky because the effort to appear casual was nearly strangling her. She didn't dare look at him, but gave him her hand just like a Brownie. He smiled in some amusement and caught it unexpectedly, turning it palm up and brushing the smooth skin with his mouth.

'Thank you, Rosslyn. I presume we return now to our former standing.'

'Why not?' she said, trembling, as nervous as a cat. 'You're the boss.'

'As long as you're sure?'

'I'm sure – and let go of my wrist. You're infallible, or near enough not to matter.'

His brilliant eyes sparkled. He was totally restored to good humour. 'I was sure you were going to like me, little one!'

'Oh, I do!' *Like* you, she thought; what a curious word when the clamour of her pulses still hadn't abated. She could even hear the sound of her own heartbeat. It was all so unreal. What she really felt for him would have to remain silent but powerful, but even silence could not reduce the after-effects of the emotional storm.

The song of a bird floated pure and silvery sweet through the trees, whether paying tribute to the moment or the spirit of the lagoon, and there had to be one, Rosslyn couldn't tell. The tumult within her, rhythmic and regular as a drumbeat, would have to be disciplined even if she could never hope to fully subdue it. She had promised herself these weeks on Belyando. It fascinated her, the timelessness, and the exotica, the voluptuousness of the tropics, the rain forest and the great galleries of ferns and palms, the magnificent crimson of the poincianas and the flame trees, the curious mammals and snakes and the glorious birdwing butterflies with a wing span of six and more inches hovering in the pink and white blossom of the bauhinias. Such space and freedom, the limitless vistas, it released and fed her already vivid imagination. Belyando was a shining reward.

Almost for a moment, with the air heavy with the incense-like perfume of the lilies, it wasn't difficult to convince herself that Boyd Ballinger was less precious to her than the land, then he caught up to her with his lithe swinging tread, and smiled down at her, rather ironically, fatalistically perhaps, either way frightening her with the delight he gave her. Then her senses were like a rising whirlwind again, moving upwards, in uproar.

She was no longer the same and no longer free to turn and run. When his hand closed over her own and his eyes slid over her face and throat, she just went along with all the latent power that was so much a part of him. Neither of them spoke all the flight back in to the homestead grounds. It was pain for Rosslyn, but strangely exquisite. She was learning and coming to life.

CHAPTER FOUR

IT was Kylie who was most keenly alive to all the life and movement on the station. Every day was just a glorious and informative nature study, with the wild bush and the lagoons a naturalist's paradise. When she was alone with Rosslyn, it was she who was the teacher, pointing out all the tracks she could interpret, the aboriginal symbols she professed to read accurately, the movements of the big herds, the advantages of certain breeds over others, the haunts of the big lizards, which Rosslyn was not eager to visit, the caves where the snakes sloughed their skins and the big yellow dingoes, the wild barkless dogs, had their lairs. She knew the biggest and best deep clear-water lagoons and just the right time to watch the brolgas, the blue cranes, turn on a display.

Kylie was an original, constantly caught up in her myriad worlds, and she did lead Rosslyn to a hide in a screen of flowering acacias to watch fifty or more brolgas in a magnificent balletic performance. Extraordinary as it seemed to the city-bred Rosslyn, it was not an uncommon sight, for the birds loved to dance — leaping high and bowing low, rushing towards one another with wings ecstatically outstretched, trumpeting in a wild and stirring mutual exchange, a staccato, far-carrying sound that Rosslyn had heard many times before, most frequently at dawn and dusk.

'Goodness, that's impressive!' she whispered in Kylie's ear.

'So are those clouds over our heads!' Kylie decided.

Rosslyn slid her hat back off her head and looked upwards. The sky did have a peculiar brassy sheen, with ominous purple clouds banking swiftly. Tropical storms were usually shortlived but very spectacular. She began dusting what she fervently hoped were twigs from the flared cuffs of her slacks. Twigs, she had found, could be anything, crawly things and spiders. 'It seems we're in for a thunderstorm. It's terribly hot, come to think of it. Here we are preoccupied with the brolgas and those clouds look violent!'

'Who cares?' Kylie asked with no proper response.

'I do, for one. We'll be soaked, and your parents are due in this afternoon. We really should get back and shower and change. You look a wreck and I know I do.'

'Oh, just stay a moment longer,' Kylie begged. 'Do you know the legend about the brolgas?'

'The one thing you haven't told me,' Rosslyn smiled.

'It must be, but I do know a little bit more about nature than you,' Kylie said kindly. 'Actually, Brolga was a young woman, a lubra, and she loved to dance. One day, she was captured by wicked cannibals . . .'

'How unsporting!'

'. . . well, *they* thought it was a fine idea. Anyway, when Brolga tried to escape, her evil tormentors, in their fury, changed her into a bird, their native companion, condemned to entertain them and dance her life away. See, Brolga is still dancing all the way down from the Dreamtime, with widespread wings. The birds never display when they're feeding, you know. You could sit here for hours then. Really, we're very lucky I'm so well informed. Look at those little lotus birds, just standing there watching. Aren't they elegant, though they must have the largest feet in the world for their size. This waterhole will be alive with birds if we do get some good rain.'

'Surely it's alive now?' Rosslyn asked in astonishment.

'Gosh, no! I've seen hundreds and hundreds more birds. They love the bulbs and the sedge and the rushes. We have the most beautiful little whistling duck in the world. Belyando's swamps have big breeding grounds, more remote than this. Uncle Boyd will have to take us. They're the ducks you hear whistling at night. They flock in thousands over the grasslands grazing like geese. The magpie geese gabble and honk and they're a real menace in the Territory.'

'Yes, I remember Humpy Doo where they wiped out the rice crop.'

'It's the waterlilies I can't get used to, for all they're as common as grass. Which ones do you like? The blue or the pink or the ivory or those big rose-coloured cups?'

'All of them. They're all beautiful. The blue are absolutely splendid – but listen, darling, time is passing and we really must get home. You know what Ellie said, you have to be completely presentable for your mother's inspection.'

'Yes, Mother sets great store by a spotless child,' Kylie said in an attacking kind of voice that set Rosslyn aback. Kylie would make a very formidable old lady.

'But you'll be pleased to see her, won't you, dear? Your father too. I mean, it's weeks now!'

'Weeks, months, years, what does it matter? This is the only kind of life I want, here on Belyando with Uncle Boyd and you. You are my true friends. My parents don't see themselves in that role!'

'Do parents have to be friends? Is that how it works? Surely no friend could approach the maternal peak, or the paternal for that matter. Parents are parents, one can't do without them, even if they don't seem to understand your world. You, for instance, have inherited your father's talent, and you've left the odd sketch around for all the ones you've hidden.'

'Careful, Rosie,' Kylie said with exquisite and funny mimicry of her uncle, 'next you'll be telling me I'll have a glorious and distinguished career.'

'Why not?' Rosslyn said quite seriously. 'You can be anything you want to be. The first lady Prime Minister of Australia, if you like. It's been done.'

'Yes, as a matter of fact it sounds very much like what I had in mind at one time, but now I've come back to nature.'

'Well, you're half-way to being an authority on that now. Get up, sweetie, your Uncle Boyd will scalp me if I don't get you home.'

'That's good!' Kylie responded in her best adult fashion. 'My Uncle Boyd wouldn't hurt a hair of your head. It's the rest of us beware!' she tacked on obscurely.

Swiftly now, plunging their heads down to avoid the whipping branches, they broke the cover of their hide. The brolgas, hearing them, were seized by great alarm. They broke their ordered ranks with dramatic speed, taking to the sky in a mad whirl, with a spatter of tiny stones on the reed flats and a powerful flap of their wings. They blackened the clouds, the sound of their anguished trumpeting almost rending the purple, silver-laced cloud masses asunder. They flew on above and before the running girls, trailing heat waves, a strangely hypnotic and wild scene that Rosslyn had difficulty in not stopping and staring at, but surely she could not hope to beat the storm in. The cloud formations were as extraordinary as atomic mushrooms and the sun piercing through one of them sent a weird ribbon of coloured light on to the deep green savannah.

A remarkably brilliant parrot gave a phenomenal screech just in front of her, and Rosslyn clapped a hand over her heart. What a fool she was! A big storm was brewing, they had only the open jeep, and Kylie was in her care. Just to make it worse, the Ballingers were arriving and Ellie had given precise instructions. A good soaking wouldn't hurt either of them, but she was frightened of lightning. It all seemed to have blown up with terrific speed. The sky had been radiantly blue and cloudless up until an hour ago. The tropics could be erratic in the extreme, she would come to know that, but she knew well enough now, lightning was dangerous to man and beast. Only the birds were flapping in the awesome dry heat and what cattle they had seen on the outward journey had made for cover in the scrub.

Breathing very quickly from their exertions, the two girls climbed into the jeep and Kylie hunted up the keys and rammed them into the ignition. The engine responded immediately and within minutes they were out of the grassland on to the dark red earthen track, almost skittling an emu who appeared from nowhere, without warning, rearing up aggressively to its full six feet, causing Rosslyn to jam on the brakes and throw out a hand to prevent Kylie being flung forward, while the emu, with incredible outraged dignity, stalked across the track, then took off in its own direction at a good thirty miles an hour. Emus often hid out from the powerful wedge-tailed eagles, but it seemed like pure suicide to race in front of a moving vehicle. The tremendous burst of speed the emu had turned on, Rosslyn well knew, could be maintained for miles, but she had no time to admire that now.

Kylie was aware of her anxiety and hastened to assure her that she didn't mind in the least being rained on. It would be fun. In fact, it might turn out to be an outstanding attraction of Rosslyn's stay. The unexpected things always were. Kylie was far from being ordinary and all kinds of thunderstorms, with or without weather, were all in a day's work. She lifted her angelic-demonic little face to the heavens, her big blue eyes glowing, and burst into some tuneful, irresponsible vocalizing.

'Raindrops are fallin' on my head . . .'

'Get down. I mean it!' Rosslyn ordered abruptly. 'Here comes the rain. One good splat at a time, then buckets. That's the least of it! It's lightning I'm worried about – and look at those jagged flashes. Get down!'

Kylie obeyed instantly, not because she thought it was the best thing to be done, but because she had a great tenderness for Rosslyn, who was visibly becoming upset. Rosslyn was so conscientious that even Ellie had been known to break out in praise. This anxiety about a 'little ole thunderstorm' was common from city slickers, when Kylie felt utterly joyous. Thunderstorms were wonderful, memorable affairs.

This one was terribly wet. Even Kylie had to concede that, and she was sorry for Rosslyn right up to the end. It must have been quite dreadful trying to drive through the pouring rain with the track throwing up the occasional waterhole. The full fury of it hit them, soaking their garments, flattening and darkening their hair, great ugly patches of red mud spattering everywhere, blowing hard against the side of the jeep and over their skin and clothes. Rosslyn, holding the wheel tightly with two hands, felt a very puny thing, but she was afraid to pull up anywhere, not with those quivering darting tongues of fire.

Just when she thought she couldn't bear it any more the rain turned off. Just like that. It might just as well have been a giant hand in charge of a tap. The driving deluge was gone and no use to look for sympathy. Kylie, straightening, took one look at Rosslyn and burst out laughing.

'Golly! You'd better take a dip for the family's sake. You look like one of the Black and White Minstrels!'

'Thanks. Have you seen yourself?'

'Well, there's no use crying about it. Ellie will be stinking.'

'They *all* will!' Rosslyn maintained with a touch of rare irritability.

'I'm certainly glad the parents aren't here. Mother has a real bite to her tongue.'

'Well, I've done my best, I guess.'

'All you *can* do!' Kylie returned piously, then let out a yelp. ' 'Struth, that's not one of ours!'

'What isn't?' Rosslyn demanded, by now thoroughly unstrung.

'That Cessna over there. That's a charter plane. *Boy!*'

The import of this dawned on them both at the same time. 'Your parents are here,' Rosslyn said, taking it right on the chin. 'We've been gone for hours and now what an entrance!'

'At least we're not drunk!'

'*Kylie*!' Rosslyn frowned at this inconsequence. 'It's my fault. I'll admit it.'

'Admit what?' Kylie asked in amazement. 'Has any harm befallen us?'

'Sheer luck!' Rosslyn said under her breath. 'We could have pitched into a big broad waterhole. In fact, we look as if we have. I've an idea — I'll drive round the back near the staff kitchens. We'll creep in like a couple of strays and Ellie will cover for us even if she does read us a lecture.'

But that was not to be. The entire household had turned out on the veranda to meet them, including the pilot of the charter flight. It was a moment for sinking through the ground. However kindly the Ballingers' attitude, they could hardly relish the sight of their only child and her foolish teacher arriving in like creatures from the lagoon. There was no distinction at all in being plastered with mud, one's shirt and slacks pasted to the skin, a normally crowning glory dark little duck tails on one's forehead and nape. However, despite everything, Rosslyn had to make a brave show or pass off a contretemps with all the aplomb of Royalty – for Kylie's sake. After all, it was quite possible that they had enjoyed themselves. Which they had, right up until the moment the rain came down and the mud threw up.

'Lord, fat chance of making a bolt for the back!' Kylie was muttering under her breath. 'And who's that with Mum? Yuck! It's that revolting Belinda something, the pipsqueak. She's in love with Uncle Boyd!'

'Another one?' queried Rosslyn.

'It happens all the time. Mother is trying to marry him off so he won't take so many chances with his life – or that's what *she* says. I think Uncle Boyd is very careful. Uncle Boyd can't risk his neck, or then we'd all be in the cart. Gee, he's not smiling or anything. None of them are. Just look at that Belinda, full of contempt.

97

I suppose she thinks we're a couple of loonies.'

'Well, let's go right up and show how intelligent we are. *Savoir-faire* is the only answer.'

'What's that?'

'That's something else again. Right-oh, sweetie, let's go up, shall we? Face the music and have done and all the rest of it. Do I look as terrible as I feel?'

'Yes.'

'It would be more tactful not to mention it. Damn!' said Rosslyn, and taking Kylie's hand she proceeded to walk around the lily pond, resisting the mad urge to catch up a gorgeous lotus flower and thrust it through her hair. Being wet, it probably wouldn't hold it. They moved on across the grass and up the short flight of steps to the veranda, the unblinking focus of many pairs of eyes.

'Nice to see you young people have enjoyed yourselves,' Boyd Ballinger drawled, his eyes gleaming like glass.

Silence from the rest of them, but hardly indifference. It was positively broody like the moments before the storm. Rosslyn longed to tell them where they could all get off, but still had the wisdom not to avail herself of the opportunity.

'I'm sorry,' she said, very sweetly and brightly, 'but we hadn't reckoned on a thunderstorm.'

'So it seems.' Sonia Ballinger spoke for the first time, completely without expression. Nevertheless she looked a perfect bitch, or so Rosslyn thought, under that pale, lofty stare. She seemed not to have the slightest desire to embrace her child, or alternatively, considering

Kylie's sodden condition, greet her by name. It was left to Boyd Ballinger to begin on the introductions, which he did very humorously and briefly, inviting Ellie to take the two little darlings off so they could shower and change. Rosslyn didn't like one moment of it.

Rick Harris, the charter pilot, seemed the only one to whom the girl's bedraggled appearance made no possible difference. Ellie's lip was drawn in, even if there was a latent sparkle somewhere in her eyes; Boyd Ballinger was sharply sardonic, faintly indulgent as usual, though Rosslyn could have slapped him, the two women Sonia and Belinda could have posed for *Vogue*, so exquisitely were they made up and groomed, and Derek Ballinger, of justified fame, and a very watered-down version of his stepbrother, had decided to remain many thousands of miles away, in spirit anyway.

It was the soggiest moment of Rosslyn's life. She tried to tell herself she would look her very best tonight for dinner and emerge victorious, but it seemed they all thought she had done it on purpose. First impressions were lasting. She would probably spend the rest of her stay apologising for her shortcomings, and as she thought this, her normal, carefree spirit turned unwontedly sober, like Ill-Fortune's darling drowning in a sea of grievances. Ellie, too, had assumed her old mantle of authority, the stern governess, shooing both girls through the house as though she could scarcely differentiate between them.

Kylie, with characteristic wilfulness, ran on ahead, her bare feet making squelchy little marks on the beautiful parquet floor, muttering under her breath, 'rotten!' and 'awful!' and something that sounded like 'skunk!'

'I'm sorry, Ellie!' Rosslyn shuddered, getting a very clear picture of her own scruffiness in a large oval mirror.

Some glimmer of amusement showed very briefly on Ellie's aristocratic, high-boned face. 'And I'll accept your apology as far as it goes. You've been gone a considerable time, Rosslyn. I did set a deadline, and up until now you've impressed me with your utter reliability.'

'Yes, I know, but I didn't engineer the storm. It was frightful, and it's shaken me up a little driving back in it. I couldn't see a foot in front of my face. We were out at the Five Mile Lagoon. The brolgas were performing and I couldn't pull myself away. I've never seen anything like it in my life. They were absolutely enchanting!'

'And it was *my* intention,' Ellie said grandly, 'that you two gels would look the same. Instead of which your duel appearance left us all with nothing to say. I did so want Kylie to make a good impression. Did anyone embrace her? Dear heaven, she's in a very odd position, that child!'

'It seems barely credible!' Rosslyn burst out wrathfully. 'No matter what, surely someone could have done that? Wet and grubby she might have been, but I can't believe it made any difference.'

'I think, Rosslyn,' Ellie responded rather heavily, 'neither of us can avoid the fact that it can and it *did*!'

'Well, I'm sorry!' Rosslyn said yet again, shaking

her wet head like a puppy. 'But I'm damned if I'm going to kiss the ground!'

'How curious, child! I don't think anyone is suggesting that.'

'Then you weren't looking at the spotless Miss Russell. I think she was rather gratified by my very droll appearance. Some kind of added pleasure!'

'Ah well!' Ellie murmured, not denying it. 'Take a shower and shampoo your hair. It should make a considerable difference. Wear that little camisole dress I like, the one with the tiered skirt. It's particularly attractive and it shows off your wonderful hair.'

'Can't I do better than that?' Rosslyn asked very seriously, determined now to reverse her earliest impression. 'I mean, it's rather ordinary, isn't it, Ellie?'

'My dear gel!' said Ellie, looking down her bony nose and speaking as though from a great height, 'though we do have our grand occasions, this is a simple dinner in the country. I've not the slightest doubt Sonia and Miss Russell will dazzle us with their magnificence, but it's far better to use just a little dash than a whole lot of cash, if I must give my view. You shall shine – Kylie too. We must, all of us, go in a forward direction. Alas, Kylie missed her big moment, but it's not as though it hasn't happened to her many times before, more's the pity, and I for one choose not to pretend any different. Am I right or am I wrong?'

'Right as usual, Ellie,' Rosslyn agreed, smiling, and on an impulse reached up and kissed Ellie's paper-dry, delicately lined cheek – a tremendous break-through in Ellie's formidable but very pleasant barriers.

For a moment it didn't seem as though Ellie was breathing. There was no doubt she was extremely surprised by Rosslyn's spontaneous and abundantly sincere gesture, then she smiled, her fine eyes lighting up and affection and approval flooding through. 'You're a good gel, Rosslyn,' she said, in a very strong and thoughtful tone, 'kind and sweet, beautiful and industrious. What more could this family want?'

'I think my virtues are all lost on them, Ellie.'

'Take heart, child!' Ellie cautioned. 'Put up a fight. I must say I was slightly annoyed to see you squelch this particular occasion, but from now on, not one opportunity should be wasted.'

This was a line quite new to Rosslyn and she peered at Ellie's face, trying to penetrate her true meaning. 'I don't know that I'm exactly with you, Ellie.'

'Then you're not using your highest level of concentration, are you, dear? Go along now, I'll see to Kylie. We can all look forward to seeing you look your best at dinner. There's no lack in your conversation, I'm pleased to say. It's excellent. I'll endeavour to transform our little Kylie. I've no doubt you both had a lovely time, but you look quite ferocious!'

In her own room, Rosslyn found this to be perfectly true. She shivered with dismay, staring at her own drowned and mud-spattered reflection with a hideous fascination. It could so easily have been different, like most things in life. She didn't care all that much for herself. She could rise above being a momentary object of ridicule – but poor little Kylie? In Rosslyn's opinion it was the Ballingers who should reproach themselves bitterly. Small wonder Kylie was immensely devoted to her uncle. He might make the head reel with all his teasing and taunts, but he was life itself with all his vitality, his force and direction and very real love for his niece – all qualities enormously emphasized by the strange apathy of his stepbrother and his stepbrother's very exclusive and cherished-looking wife, if only by herself. Many long hours and a whole lot of work would have to go into that totally indulged, richly elegant charisma.

On the other hand, Derek Ballinger had little of Boyd's unique and very devastating physical vibrancy. His voice was soft, not crisp with an edge to it, his tall, very thin body lacked the lithe co-ordination and casual throwaway elegance, the family resemblance was fairly obvious in bone structure and the midnight black hair but not the colour-changing eyes. Kylie's eyes were her father's, a clear blue. Boyd's were a brilliant gold flecked blue-green. Boyd had an uncontrived air of authority he had worn for most of his life. Derek gave the overwhelming impression that he was a man of many difficulties, one step ahead of retiring to absolute seclusion where he had the time and the scope to concentrate all his energies on the one thing that really mattered to him – his work.

Derek Ballinger had come into life different. His mother, who had always recognized it, had somehow managed to remarry into the still lingering French aristocracy and gone off to live in France. His father, dead now, and for Derek perhaps fortunately, had ridiculed his artistic aspirations and tried to turn him into a second-class Boyd. There was only one Boyd and they all knew it. His wife, Sonia, was very generous with her time and did honestly try to please him. His daughter Kylie baffled and perplexed him. Indeed he had great difficulty realizing she was his, only she was so surely a Ballinger. It was a kind of cruelty for Derek to get through life at all, save for his painting, and not even then. Some days everything was a torment when he just wanted to run and hide, and today was one of them.

All these things Rosslyn was to find out by just being what she was, very beautiful and charming and a shade too tender-hearted herself. Life was just full of emotional entanglements and it needed no great observational qualities to realize this. With Kylie, Derek Ballinger was to embark on his most serious and ambitious work, but strangely this was to make nobody happy. Derek had come to Belyando to rest on his brother's strength, to draw peace and comfort from it. Boyd had always supported him, even when he was the very rawest material, a spiritually struggling art student with his father shut away from him in utter disgust and Boyd preparing to mount the throne. He had looked and felt in those days persecuted and exhausted, and he didn't look or feel very much different now, but Boyd was towering in stature, the cattle baron, pretty much as their father had been, except that Boyd had a heart to counterbalance the ruthless man of destiny.

Boyd had never called him a melodramatic idiot! in a hard resonant voice with a curling lip. Boyd was infinitely kinder than their father had been, but no handsomer. Boyd was the living spit of him. It was disconcerting until Derek saw the sympathy and understanding in his brother's eyes. Nevertheless their father would be continually between them. Boyd was everything a man could wish for in a son, Derek, sensitive to the point of suffering, vulnerable to every harsh word and mocking gibe. Even Ellie in their childhood had tried to infuse into him a little of Boyd's tremendous spirit and daring. It hadn't worked, as his father took a grim pleasure in pointing out. Ellie never gave up, but Derek had remained a thorn in his father's side until the day he died. Even to this day, for all his success he had only to hear echoes of his father's voice, look into Boyd's eyes in the big portrait in the library, to feel a weak fool.

The only real peace Derek knew in his heart was that there could never be such a final and inevitable breach between himself and his brother. Boyd was their father at his best, with a greater urbanity and generosity. Boyd was Boyd, the only single one of his relations Derek didn't find incomprehensible and detestable. If his opinions were laughed at by the rest of the family who supported him to a degree, they nevertheless went very deep with Derek. His was a very impressionable and self-revolving temperament with no solid core of strength nor even a balancing sense of humour. Derek had a taste for heroics, but his artistic eye was exquisitely refined. It was necessary always to express himself in this way, and Rosslyn, as Boyd Ballinger had so early betrayed with such diverting irony, was remarkably paintable, as radiant as a flower with magical colouring and a rare emotional quality. As a model she would be ideal, but whether she would prove a wise choice or not remained to be seen.

CHAPTER FIVE

If Rosslyn was to develop into the sort of woman who would look at home anywhere, Sonia and Belinda visibly lacked this amazing versatility. They were, first and last, creatures of the *haute monde*, totally geared to urban life, a life of amusements and pleasure, seasoned travellers of the jet set, and the jet set didn't normally take to the wilds. This Rosslyn found good to know. Furthermore, though they looked wonderful but rather chastely elegant against this exotic, tropical background, they had, up to date, appeared as silent and lifeless as moon goddesses.

It was Ellie who held court, Ellie with her thick white hair magnificently coiled in a hitherto unseen Edwardian style, spare and impressive in an ancient but timeless purple gown, with a fantastic gold mask pendant swinging from her throat. She was talking very intelligently and animatedly in her impeccable accent about Ancient Egyptian culture, *her* subject, at that particular moment, the step pyramid of King Zoser. She mentioned his name as casually with the fixed idea everyone would know him as well as the late King of England, and it was left to Rosslyn, who had been a good student of Ancient History, to pass on the information that King Zoser had been the great and powerful king of the Old Kingdom, which put him three thousand years B.C.

It was all the same to Ellie but not so to Sonia and Belinda, who looked pained and unimpressed, and Rick Harris the charter pilot, who was understandably lost in a civilization so long gone. Boyd Ballinger, of course, was used to these shattering discussions, though he often indicated a time limit, but Derek Ballinger seized on it as though he had been waiting for just such a subject all his life, unexpectedly launched into orbit. He had the bit between his teeth now, moving across to the Aegean and the classical Greeks, *his* subject, fathoms deep in structure and form, their perfect architecture, their perfect everything and just about everyone else's profound ignorance. He was extraordinarily stimulated, his blue eyes for once blazing, and lighting, to Rosslyn's growing astonishment, most often on her.

She hadn't the slightest idea of Derek Ballinger's intense awareness and love of natural beauty that would have done any ancient Greek proud. She only realized, minute by minute, that the sight of her was meriting some ardent critical acclaim, an *entente cordiale* of eyes. She should have been flattered, but she was made to feel moderately uneasy. The beautiful chandelier above their heads, had she known it, had brought her to glittering life – her skin and her hair, her golden, almond eyes, the sheen of the bronze silk in her simple camisole dress cut low and straight in the front with narrow straps across her smooth, satiny shoulders. Ellie had given her an Art Nouveau necklace ('too erotic for me') and the rare yellow garnets glowed in a curved frame of gold. She appeared at that moment like a model Renoir would have pounced upon, lighting up her surroundings, a fascinating medley of delicacy and charm and shimmering clean colour and light.

It all added to the unexpectedness of the situation and no one at the dinner table was proving a detached observer. Rick Harris, too, was staring at Rosslyn as though she had in the past hour performed some kind of woman magic. In fact her entrance for pre-dinner drinks had confounded them all, with the exception of Boyd Ballinger, who merely looked suavely pensive, and Ellie who gave a gratified smile and accepted Rosslyn into her own charmed circle. All this with some justification, for she looked as softly dazzling as morning sunlight, making Belinda muffle a horrified gasp. No attractive woman wished to be outclassed, and to make it worse, Rosslyn was proving amusing and interesting too. Even, of all things, with the courage to challenge that old dragon Ellie's dating of some obscure Hittite monument, whatever that was. Altogether, Belinda's fine, straight nose was being bent out of joint. Sonia's too, but not to the same degree, for Sonia had a husband, and Belinda was on Belyando looking for one. Sonia had never wanted a demanding husband in any case, so Derek suited her rather well.

It was Belinda who most bitterly resented the focusing, unfairly, of the limelight. It was quite a feather in her cap to know she was a constant source of attraction to most men she met, but none of the men, for the moment, appeared to be noticing her. Boyd, the cool devil, a quirk to his mouth, was looking intrigued and satirical and amused all at once, Derek was babbling on endlessly from the dawn of time, and Rick Harris, though very attractive in a gangly sunbleached blond fashion, simply didn't have enough 'change' to step up in line. And here, Belinda was being very shortsighted, for Rick Harris in later years was to head a thriving internal airline.

'Rubbish!' Ellie cried, her patience sorely tried by something Derek was saying. 'You're a dreamer!' she added trenchantly.

'That's my belief as well, but he's brilliant, Ellie, please don't forget!' Boyd Ballinger looked down at Ellie and smiled. 'Can we continue this compelling epic quarrel at another time? Sonia and Belinda are receiving all this with mixed reactions and a couple of stifled yawns.'

'Not to say me!' Rick Harris grinned. 'Who's this bloke Theodorus of Phocaea anyway?'

'A big name in architecture about the fourth century B.C.,' Rosslyn explained cheerfully.

'Thank you, Miss Marshall.'

'Rosslyn,' she smiled at him, and Rick smiled back.

Impatient of this development, Derek Ballinger broke in. 'I wonder if I could persuade you, Rosslyn, to sit for me.'

She blinked as though at the unimaginable and Boyd Ballinger laughed out loud, his gleaming eyes ranging all over her face and shoulders and back to the dancing red and rose amber highlights on the tips of her silken curls. Involuntarily her heart leapt in desire, but Derek was fighting for her attention with unbridled frustration.

'Well?'

'I'd be honoured – I mean that. I admire your work tremendously.'

'There you are! Is that enough?' Boyd looked across to his stepbrother.

Derek subsided, eyeing Rosslyn avidly. As a prospective model, she was having the most striking impression on him – her skin and her hair, the texture and colour, the great golden eyes so piquantly tiptilted, the composite picture spurring him to new heights. Indeed it was difficult for him to sit still, he never ate much anyway and the whole idea for a full-length portrait was clarifying by the second with a completeness and wholeness that overjoyed him and brought his artistic heart right into his mouth. Rosslyn at that moment wasn't a young woman to him, most certainly not his young daughter's teacher and companion, but a creature of visual excitement, an artistic impetus, and she had to be confined to canvas, otherwise he would be unable to rest. He stifled a groan and Boyd, damn him, laughed again, sounding for a moment almost like their father.

Rosslyn too, he noticed, flushed under Boyd's very green gaze, but this time Derek was sure of himself. This girl positively inspired him, and not everyone could do that, not even in a world full of beautiful women. It was all a matter of light. Derek was preoccupied with light and a world of multiple sensations.

Sonia, for instance, whose looks were much admired, had the cool, static beauty of starlight. It chilled him now and then. This girl was the sun, from the flamelike curls of her hair, radiating out in short little bursts like glittering rays to the smooth, satin-textured gloss of her skin, a surface that reflected the light and created illusions with colour. Sonia and Belinda too seemed vaguely blue to him, or they did beside this girl. His vision was so clear to him it was almost explosive. The most important thing that seemed to have happened to him in a long while. Five years at least and it would be a kind of experiment. Posterity would know him. Even his father might get to know of it if he lived on some extra-terrestrial plane.

'Well, that's splendid, then!' Boyd was saying, further buoying him up. Boyd too seemed to be lavishing consummate critical faculties on his model. 'It's a good thing, Derek, you've never been lured into social portraiture where you more or less have to flatter your sitter. Derek's art, Rosslyn,' he explained, looking right at her, 'is solely concerned with free expression. In this case, you're both lucky. I'm almost persuaded to start enthusing myself!'

Money, the essential commodity, wasn't even considered at all, and thinking this Rick Harris, who was up to his ears in financial troubles, gave a wry smile to himself. Lucky devils! Boyd he had known for a year or more, ever since he had started out on this charter flight thing. Boyd had helped a lot and Boyd he liked very much. Ballinger was a man who never expected or asked it, but he seemed to command everyone's respect and admiration as a matter of course.

Derek, the stepbrother, didn't seem to fall into this category at all. It was hard to realize he was Boyd's brother at all, except for obvious physical similarities. Famous as he was supposed to be, he was a completely unfamiliar type to Rick, seemingly locked away in some curious world of his own, raving on about antiquities, not even Helen of Troy, but devouring Rosslyn with far from glacial blue eyes, but not intensely male either. For all his malices and miseries and he appeared to be saturated in them, Rick was sure the worry about money had never obtruded on Derek Ballinger's struggle to the top. The Ballingers, he knew as well as the next man, ran a kind of empire of their own, but Boyd and Belyando seemed to be a big source of their power and Boyd took the total pressure of running this great station, no easy thing, and he had had his setbacks, though he was the most vital human being Rick had ever known.

Two brothers. Two different worlds. Different mothers, of course. Did that explain it? Rick thought. Women usually explained everything. He gazed across at Rosslyn as the foremost woman on his mind at the moment. Even drenched and densely mud-spattered, she had impressed him, and her marked sense of the ridiculous. Her feeling had been for the child, he could see that. Curious parents. They might have arrived in a space ship, so exceedingly oddly had they reacted to the sight of their only child. A pretty little thing too – stuck her tongue out at him just as she got in through the door. He hadn't realized some parents acted that

113

way with their offspring. His own mother hugged him and kissed him to this day. The teacher, Rosslyn, had a lovely figure, very slender but obviously deliciously and delicately curved. Rick's eye, richly encouraged by the amount of wine he had drunk over dinner, fell to details, until, needing a breathing space, he encountered Boyd's spiked, satirical stare, grinned and looked away.

What chance did he stand if Boyd Ballinger fancied *la belle Rozalene*? No woman in her right mind would compare them. Ballinger had it made, rich and virile and extravagantly classy. The worst part was, Rick liked him. In quick succession, Rick the extrovert and exuberant young man fell to studying the others. This dinner at Belyando was a first for him and he was making the most of it. The homestead was a dream, chock-a-block with valuable things but marvellously liveable-in and comfortable. The old lady, Miss Eleanor, was clearly an eccentric, some kind of Victorian extravaganza, in an absurd fusty old dress redolent of mothballs, and what looked like a crude gold object swinging round her neck. Everyone knew that so far as Ballinger was concerned Miss Eleanor was one of Belyando's attractions, so Rick remembered to treat her with respectful formality, or as much as he could manage which wasn't a great deal, but he wasn't to know that. Not for him the curious delight and amusement that Ballinger and even Rosslyn, who could only have been twenty, not the old lady's vintage at all, seemed to be getting from all Miss Eleanor's clipped and high-flown statements.

The other two, Mrs. Sonia Ballinger and her friend from the big city, Miss Belinda Russell, just reeked of money and all it could buy – a world just turned on for them. Both of them were good-lookers, though not so appetizing as the delectable Miss Marshall. Mrs. Ballinger was a particularly cool blonde and the tall Belinda was a splendid foil, which was why they gravitated together: an experienced, dark-golden-tanned brunette, fluttering her thick black lashes in Ballinger's direction, fiery points of light in the depths of her dark eyes, and who could blame her? But this provocative and pulsating pose was apparently lost on Boyd, at least for the time being, as the imperious old Miss Eleanor, who acted more like a favoured maiden aunt than just an old governess, decided for all of them it would be nice to have coffee and liqueurs on the cool jasmine-scented verandah.

Much later that night, Rosslyn lay awake for a long time. She had a lot to think about and she was thinking hard. Not so very many minutes before, some sound from the garden, a woman's laugh, a bird? had disturbed her and she had got out of bed quickly and looked out of the window over the moon-dappled darkness. Two figures loomed out of the shadows, arm in arm, obviously in harmony, strolling back towards the house with all the time in the world. The sound came again, a ripple of gaiety with sensuous overtones. One figure was unmistakably Boyd, his height, the width of shoulder, the set of his head and his lithe co-ordination; the other was Belinda, long hair swinging, her glamorous white silk jersey rather ghostly in the moonlight.

She was having a brilliant time benefiting from everyone else's disappearance. Belinda had made a few promises to herself. One of them was Boyd Ballinger, and it was urgent. She just didn't want a love affair or a pleasant invitation. She was twenty-nine and though her best days were far from over she was anxious to get on with marriage. Boyd Ballinger had always held her. He made her excited and nervous. Boyd had been a long-term enterprise. She had known the Ballingers for years, Sonia was her friend and Sonia had worked hard to bring her friend and her brother-in-law together. Sonia was an excellent influence, or so Belinda thought. At the end of this lovely long week, providing the red-headed schoolteacher didn't ruin her chances, or put other minor difficulties in her way, Belinda hoped to make a welcome announcement. Tonight was real progress. Boyd hadn't neglected her despite the meddling of the elderly Miss Eleanor.

Carefully Rosslyn withdrew from the window, although no one could possibly see her. She felt strangely chilled and disturbed, though she might have expected it after all those dark-eyed ravenous glances over dinner and afterwards. She wasn't jealous – she had no right to be. She was a woman; so was Belinda. How could she blame Belinda if the older girl was more enterprising? Nevertheless she had a strong tendency to cry. Boyd Ballinger was irresistible, a seething whirlpool of dangerous excitement. One could only expect emotional upsets with a man like that around.

She hurried back quickly and flung herself into the big fourposter bed like a child who had stumbled on an enormous, double-dealing secret, pulling the soft boronia-scented sheet over her head, desperately trying not to make herself miserable. If Belinda wanted to go for a midnight stroll with Boyd Ballinger she was welcome. If it came to that, there was no good reason why they shouldn't marry . . . *except* . . . Boyd had told her quite emphatically that he wasn't prepared to take on the extra responsibility of a wife. But then they all said that. Sometimes a man couldn't avoid it. There was always the woman with whom a man couldn't trust himself, despite his better judgment. If she was that kind of woman herself, the thought hadn't occurred to her. Belinda, now, was very chic and worldly, with a glossy, fashionable sophistication. She was no intellectual, but men were scrupulous about avoiding intellectual women unless they had the sense to keep it well hidden.

Ellie, now, was the first to admit that her academic brilliance had thoroughly unnerved what few suitors she had in her youth. Ellie thrived, then and now, on controversial subjects and academic battles. It was a mistake, and one Belinda never made. Her appeal was mostly sexual and she didn't neglect any aspect of it, then too she was very shrewd and efficient in the matters that affected her. As Boyd Ballinger's good-looking, pampered wife she would make sure her own way of life wouldn't be threatened to an intolerable degree. The womenfolk of wealthy station owners had the whole world as their oyster, all kinds of exclusive backgrounds against which they could indulge themselves when station life became too dreary or lonely.

One need only strike out for the big cities. A few weeks here and there made all the difference.

So far as Rosslyn was concerned Belyando *was* the whole wide wonderful world at her door. She would never want it to be any different. And Boyd! At the thought of him heat swept her slight body. She was even a little panic-stricken by her increasing pre-occupation with him. It was growing inside her like some devouring flower, spreading giant petals to the very ends of her nervous system. She should never have let him kiss her. Then again, what a fool she would have been to miss such an experience. Being able to kiss, she had found, was as much a gift as being able to play the piano, where one's performance depended a great deal on the quality of the instrument. Boyd was brilliant. The most critical woman could find no fault with him, unless he was inclined to forget one's existence for days at a time. Nevertheless he was winning all the time. But why, *why?* Was it fascination, infatuation, a headlong physical response? Her feelings went a whole lot deeper than that, like fiery, iridescent cart-wheels exploding in the soft, purple darkness. She either had to go home or do something about herself. Apparently she had aroused some suspicion in Belinda's svelte breast, aptly illustrated by the number of feline, narrow-eyed, summing-up glances that had been directed towards her, but always with extreme caution. The Ballingers put such store on good manners, and bad manners, admittedly, were ugly and embarrassing. Still, a plain warning had been issued. *'Don't let anything develop. He's mine!'*

What nonsense! Nobody really belonged to anyone else. Boyd Ballinger was a free spirit and he always would be one, even if he went suddenly overboard and took nine wives. The thing to do was to get out while she could still maintain the illusion that he was no more to her than Kylie's uncle and a wonderful host. Kylie would miss her, of course, but her parents were here now and surely they had to come around in time. Sonia had already stirred herself to ask one or two pertinent questions and she had seemed to hang on the answers. It had been an encouraging sign after such a difficult start. But no, there was this painting! Derek Ballinger had assured her it would be important, outstanding, looking into her face very much like Kylie about to cry if she said no.

With her eyes tightly closed, Rosslyn willed up another face – vivid, darkly handsome, eyes neither blue nor green, a mocking smile on the clear-cut mouth, a deep cleft in the chin; did *that* make him jealous? Probably he had the knack for overcoming any extravagant tendencies. He had a sensuous nature anyway and a faultless technique. No wonder Belinda was enjoying herself. She, Rosslyn, was in much too deep. For all her physical beauty she was essentially a one-man woman. Now she was very serious and shaken and very oddly subject to recurrent dreams, something that had never happened to her before. They were all about the same thing – Boyd. Love should really make people laugh, instead of which she was lying awake fretting with the mosquitoes zooming over her head and the net not pulled to come to her rescue. In coming to Belyando she had turned her life upside down, and she had to take the full blame. She had known that from just the sound of his voice.

The very next morning, Derek Ballinger got under way with work on the portrait. Whatever other upsets life had to offer, his painting gave him greatly fluctuating bursts of satisfaction, when joy and power and intensity descended like a curtain blocking off the outside world. As he told Boyd and Sonia, he was quite certain he had made an important decision and he was showing more than a little of his father's abhorred ruthlessness in attaining his own ends. There had been rather a distressing little incident with Kylie before breakfast. Kylie was never at her best when her father was around, and now it was patent that he intended depriving her of her friend and a wonderful companion on all her nature study jaunts. To be specific, she had only just discovered the dearest little family of agile wallabies in one of the pandanus thickets, and not two hundred yards away but very well camouflaged, a batch of beautiful dark green emu eggs – eight. Apparently the male emu who did most of the brooding had wandered off for a break from nearly two months of incubation, and inquisitive Kylie had investigated the nest.

At the very least out of this mild scene her uncle was afforded the opportunity of warning her away from the nest. A broody emu could very well choose to turn nasty. Instead, by way of compensation, he put her on the track of the spotted bower bird which one of the coloured boys claimed he had seen in an enormous fig tree about eight miles to the south-east. Melly, their most trusted house girl and an excellent horsewoman, bushwoman and shot, was detailed to accompany her. This morning Rosslyn could not be spared; besides, the bower bird was an extraordinary mimic, faithfully reproducing a wide variety of bird sounds outside its own species, a plain little brown bird for most of the time, collecting all kinds of bright objects, mostly red or white, and in the presence of a female turning on a series of displays when it flared its pink-into-violet neck feathers into a gorgeous fan. This was the moment Kylie and Melly might have the good fortune to witness, and why didn't Kylie take her camera along? It had cost enough, and Kylie was an accomplished amateur photographer.

Rosslyn had tried to buoy her along, smiling repeatedly across the breakfast table, but Kylie was not to be mollified and showed shades of her old mulishness. Just to top it off Sonia Ballinger had come in and proceeded to take Kylie to task for not brushing her hair. She had, but not, as she put it, 'a crazy and unnecessary hundred strokes!' Such a piece of impertinent back-answering inevitably led to further disasters and Kylie was sent from the room, hurling her chair backwards in the process as a perfect example of what little progress Rosslyn had made as a strict and healthy-minded mentor. Belinda was positively sneering over her black coffee, nibbling at a wafer-thin piece of dry toast.

Derek Ballinger thrust back his chair and got up

from the table in utter contempt, signalling to Rosslyn that she was to go before him. The only possible thing she *could* do was to walk out, leaving her second cup of coffee unfinished, and a less than sunny atmosphere behind her.

In the large, light-filled, airy room set aside as Derek's studio when he was in residence, Rosslyn sat very still and tried not to swallow or fidget or shift her feet. She didn't feel at all happy or at home with Derek, which was rather odd considering that Boyd and Kylie were basically as fellow human beings very familiar to her. Derek was decidedly different. If there was a highly coloured and often erroneous image in the public mind of the dedicated artist, it was he. In fact, in his own way he was very funny, scowling ferociously at the propped-up canvas, but his right hand, with a dynamic life of its own, worked in the most disciplined and economic way. There was a constant, barely heard, and not meant to be, commentary to each stage of his progress, which just went to show how deeply involved he was, like Kylie breathing hard over one of her masterpieces with the tip of her tongue caught firmly between her teeth.

Rosslyn as a woman simply didn't exist for him at all. She was a beautiful object, and he made this point clear with his quite shocking dissecting look, like a great surgeon with clear unblinking eyes. It would have been the source of great unease to an uninitiated model, but no great puzzlement to Rosslyn, who had attended art classes herself, as part of her course, and had a not insignificant degree of drawing ability herself.

'You're bored. I'm making you nervous?'

His voice, though very soft and refined, nearly made her jump out of her skin. It had been a good forty minutes since he had so addressed her directly and she had gone into a trance of her own.

'A little stiff, maybe!' she said, rallying. 'May I see?'

'Certainly not!' he said snappily, not trifling to hide his annoyance. 'There'll be plenty of time. Plenty!' He picked up a rag and wiped a dab of paint from his forehead. Younger than Boyd, he gave the impression that he was very much older and worn. Not a physical thing, for he was handsome enough with the Ballinger bone structure, but a pressured, nervous, I'm-almost-at-the-end-of-my-strength. 'At least you don't try to chat. That I just could not stand. Mostly to please Sonia and because she takes care of me so well, I did a quick portrait of Belinda a year or two ago. I nearly went out of my mind. No idle statement, the threat was real. Belle tries to vamp every man she sees – even me!'

'Why even you? You're a very attractive man, Mr. Ballinger, unless you mean you're married and very virtuous about it.'

'My dear young lady,' he said mildly, 'every man is a bachelor out of his wife's sight!'

'I don't believe that.'

'You should.'

'Some never forget, surely?'

'Well, as a matter of fact, now that you mention it, *I* don't. I leave all the fascinating women to Boyd. Much the better man. I've always wanted to paint him, you know, a wonderfully stimulating subject. There's a great deal to Boyd. He's a very strong and complex man, but I can't get him to sit still for five minutes. Always Belyando, the same old story. It won't run away.'

'Maybe the cattle might. Tempe Downs had that incident of cattle duffing, and I heard Boyd ask Rick Harris to keep his eyes open on his way back to Cairns. Belyando is so big, I daresay a gang could get away with a few hundred head.'

'Well, that's something I just read about in the papers!' Derek retorted in a very bored voice, and Rosslyn realized he hadn't the slightest interest in the admininstration of the station. If the station put the butter on his bread, it was one small detail he could afford to overlook. He was, she thought, with no sense of surprise, rather incredibly self-centred and he had a dauntless strength of his own. It occurred to her too that his brother Boyd would make ten of him – to look at, to live with, to rely upon. No revelation, most people felt the same. But Derek was brilliant as a painter and his gift was real.

'What about that picture of Boyd in the small drawing-room, the one when he was a boy?' It was a favourite of Rosslyn's and she often stole in to look at it, but naturally wasn't going to admit that to anyone except Kylie, who often did the same.

Derek was frowning hard as though searching his memory, when he was really only hurtling himself back in time. 'Our father commissioned that,' he said flatly. 'His word was law and Boyd was the adored heir.'

'It's a wonderful portrait.'

'Yes, it's good. Boy into man. He was about thirteen then, handsome, daring, very self-sufficient, enterprising, good at everything – a paragon. I had a hard time following Boyd through boarding school. I was always Boyd Ballinger's brother. I don't think I ever rated my own name, and to make matters worse I was a complete washout on the sports field where Boyd positively starred. Very depressing. I can't bear to think of my boarding school years – a purgatory, but better than being at home. Do *you* know the way to stand clear of a man's shadow? First a father, then a brother!'

'It seems to me,' she said crisply, 'you've made a very illustrious name of your own.'

'I suppose I have and it should be flattering, but it isn't. Perhaps, as they say, one can never throw off the effects of one's childhood.'

Exactly, she thought. Which is why you should be paying a great deal more attention to Kylie, a parallel example. 'My childhood was very happy,' she said, feeling rather hot under the collar, and a flush stained her skin, making her eyes glow brilliantly.

'Don't I know it!' he answered, narrowing his eyes at her, then returning them to the canvas. 'You have a very radiant quality. You're good and you're beautiful, better still, you're kind. One can see it in your face. Generosity and compassion are very necessary qualities in a woman. When a woman is without them she's only a caricature of herself, often cruel. I detest cruel women, and there are so many of them about!'

'Have you ever painted one?'

'Good God, no. That would be immoral!'

And that settled that!

Kylie still wasn't back by lunchtime, and afterwards the porcelain-skinned Sonia, in a dashing pull-on hat, sunglasses, a silk blouse in Paris motifs to her wrists, sky blue slacks, a little bit of skin peeping through the wide straps of her sandals, took to a series of long, frosty drinks, lazing in the combined shade of the octagonal pool house and the big striped umbrella, watching a very sportive Belinda sun and swim in spectacular little scraps of coffee and white jersey that went under the courtesy name of swimsuit. It was the sort of bikini only the woman who dared would think of, and Belinda dared rather better than most people, judging from her deep all-over suntan. Then, too, her figure was near perfect, tall and athletic, with wide shoulders, a deep, beautiful bosom of which she was inordinately proud, a small waist, trim hips and derriere and long, sleek legs. She was anyone's idea of an eyeful and Rosslyn scarcely knew how Boyd could tear himself away to chase dingoes. But he did, and took them all by surprise.

Rosslyn hurried after him, throwing all restraint to the winds. 'Boyd?'

'What now?' He halted, twisting his dark head to look over his shoulder.

'May I come?'

'How so?' One black eyebrow shot up in a brisk unreassuring fashion. 'I'm going to shoot the damned things! Aren't you squeamish?'

'I suppose it's necessary?' she asked breathlessly.

'Such a damned fool question! Do you think I go around killing for the fun of it? Have you ever seen a slaughtered calf? Not a pretty sight. The dingoes are a real menace in the rougher country, culling the weaker cattle. Their numbers have to be strictly controlled.'

'No need to snap my head off.'

For a second his brilliant opal-coloured eyes swept over her with special awareness. 'I'm sorry, baby! You want to come, let's go!'

Still she stood staring as though riveted to the spot. 'Why did you call me baby?'

'Because that's what you look like sometimes,' he bit off impatiently. 'Especially beside Belinda.'

'You can say that again!' she said guardedly. 'I wouldn't have so much oomph ten thousand years from now.'

'Don't undersell yourself. You're perfect in your way, but you're first and foremost fragile, not a frontierswoman. Are you sure about this? I haven't the time, forget the inclination, to hold your hand and act nursemaid. There's a job to be done.'

'I can look after myself,' she said earnestly.

'No, you can't!'

'Why not?' she asked with dignity, smarting under that mere lick of contempt.

'You're not clever enough.'

She shrugged and glanced away from his exasperating expression, a mixture of great charm and arrogance. 'I guess that's true. On Belyando anyway!'

'Naturally,' he turned and smiled at her averted profile, 'which is not to say everywhere. I realize that, Rosslyn, so don't look so outraged. I don't mean to hurt you intentionally.'

'Well, it's well within your grasp!'

'Would you rather I didn't hurt you, and why, particularly, can I?'

His brilliant eyes were challenging her, leading her deeper and deeper into some web of his making. 'Let it pass!' she said, giving a rapid shake of her head.

'I have to,' he said tersely, 'but the time will come, Rosslyn, when I'll raise the question again.'

She took a deep breath of clean, sweet air, trying to anaesthetize herself from his spell – this man, this Boyd Ballinger with his fine blaze of power, a bred-in-the-bone arrogance, and a lean, hard frame. Sunlight and shade from the canopy of tangled green played over his dark face. He looked enormously vital and daring, full of a rare confidence and energy. A man's environment had a tremendous effect on him, just as it affected all forms of life. This world of the tropics and the rain forest was fantastic, very colourful and luxurious, a true sensory experience. Boyd Ballinger exactly fitted his environment. It was his birthright, a flowering, wild kingdom.

He checked in his stride to look down at her poignant, rather curious expression. 'All right, all right, all right!' he said as though amused and relenting. 'Let's make one last attempt to be friends. I'd like to, especially with your mouth in that delicious soft pout. I'd dearly like to kiss it, but I daren't!'

'Why not? Belinda isn't watching!' she said rashly.

'I don't like that!' he said, his challenging eyes staring her down, demanding an apology.

'I'm sorry,' she murmured, obliging. 'I don't like it either. Did you enjoy your midnight tour of the garden?' she asked with soft urgency.

'Yes, I did!' he said rather brutally, flicking her a leashed look. 'Did you want to come too? Poor little Rosslyn, with the enormous tawny eyes. Normally I would have taken you, but Belinda likes a man's undivided attention.'

'That's the answer all right!'

'Don't all women demand too much of a man's time? What's all this about anyway?' he demanded, surrendering to irritation. 'Go and put your riding gear on. I'll give you ten minutes exactly, then your time has run out.'

'I'll be back in eight!' she promised, whirling about, her rose-amber curls glittery in the sunlight.

No answer from him, nor a change in his rather formidable expression. He turned and stalked away from her with his peculiarly noiseless tread, as though he considered, in his wisdom, reversing his decision. Women were trouble, no new discovery. The thought was implicit in the set of his wide, powerful shoulders.

CHAPTER SIX

BELINDA, who had gone through the process of falling in love a dozen or more times, knew every sign, every step on the way, consequently it was no longer possible for her to remain silent or cope with the awful strain on her nerves. The redheaded schoolteacher was a positive threat, her influence in the household quite harmful. Sonia and she had spoken of it together (Sonia seemed to guess all her thoughts) and it had been agreed, without being too hard on the girl, for she was very good with Kylie, that Belinda must establish her territorial rights before her nerves got the better of her.

Belinda wasn't exactly happy about it. It was an outrage having any competition at all, but good lord, it was necessary.

Both women realized simultaneously, as was their way, that something was radically wrong when Boyd and Rosslyn together with young Kylie had come in from an orchid-gathering excursion into the rain forest. They looked a diabolically close trio, almost a unit, Boyd so darkly handsome, faintly indulgent, Rosslyn with her delicate flower face illuminated by the sparks of love she so rightly reproached herself for not being able to hide, Kylie, a mine of information on natural hybridization and the immense chemical potential of a handful of little plants, beaming on both adults as very special people she could not be without.

For the first time for a long time, Sonia searched her own conscience, and came up with a few gaps. She would have to pay more attention to her own child or run the risk of losing her affection. Smitten by the justice of this, Sonia had jumped to her feet with enormous awareness and fired at her daughter a flatering questionnaire, seeing herself on the brink of a wonderful new relationship. Parents, after all, were meant to take the initiative.

Belinda, deserted, tried to remain calm. She was a realist, but she soon made some excuse to follow Rosslyn to her room. The very last thing she wanted was a vulgar confrontation, but the vision of Boyd and Rosslyn together was still burning brightly in painfully sharp detail. It had altered the position quite drastically. She had never thought of Boyd as actually her own property (what woman could?) but damn it all, she had a great deal more right to him than any piquant-faced schoolteacher. Belinda was deeply attached to the Ballingers, and to lose Boyd was to lose everything.

She was by no means helpless. She had Sonia as a powerful ally, and the girl looked a simple, good-natured creature, sweet and sensitive, the type who couldn't withstand scenes. Belinda could withstand anything for Boyd. She was a mature woman, well versed in these matters, and Rosslyn didn't stand a chance. To delay would be to let the position worsen every day. The girl was quite young and distressingly pretty and she had to be warned off Belinda's future husband. The fact that Boyd had neglected to ask her to marry him conveniently slipped Belinda's mind. Boyd wouldn't be the first man to wake up and find himself engaged. Christmas, the festive season, seemed appropriate, and at least Boyd knew the family he would be marrying into. The Russells were notorious for marrying well, and Belinda, like the rest of her family, could be ruthless and infinitely calculating.

There was no one in the hallway when she went down to Rosslyn's room, so she knocked on the door, waiting for the sound of Rosslyn's attractive, friendly voice calling: 'Come in.'

'Miss Marshall?' Belinda threw open the door, tall and confident, her autocratic dark gaze on the slight graceful figure in the centre of the room. 'I hope I'm not disturbing you, but I thought we might have a chat.'

'Right now?' Rosslyn asked, completely losing her look of dreamy introspection and assuming a very alert manner, both adult and full of wry comprehension.

It took Belinda wholly by surprise, deficient as she was in her assessment of Rosslyn's true character. 'Any reason why not?' she retorted aggressively.

'I thought I might wash my hair before dinner. It's full of little bits of fern and twig and I'm sure a record number of little winged things. Our rain forests don't only have the greatest collection of primitive plants in the world! Won't you sit down? I feel you have something to say to me. I'm right, aren't I?' Rosslyn turned away to the dressing table and picked up a brush, whirling her hair into the most incredible silken disorder that only succeeded in making her look more mysterious than ever, like a rare flower with a fresh, seductive appeal; a natural fragrant feminine essence that no amount of effort and experimenting could achieve.

Belinda shook her own long dark hair back so that it rippled away from her face and crossed her long, shapely legs with precision. She could scarcely bear to look at the other girl's undoubted beauty. It had no virtue at all in her eyes. Paintings and objets d'art were the things to be cherished. 'I've agonized about this ...' she began untruthfully.

'Surely it doesn't deserve it?'

'I don't know what you're talking about,' Belinda said shortly, 'and I certainly didn't come here to listen to your facetious comments.'

'Then perhaps you'll tell me what you *are* here for, seeing it's not going to be pleasant.'

'All right! My plans!' Belinda snapped, in a hard, projecting tone.

'I've heard of them!' Rosslyn said irresistibly.

Belinda searched her face, oddly disconcerted. 'I hate to say this, Miss Marshall, but I don't think I like you.'

'Aren't I being as co-operative as I should be, or alternatively as ... tractable?'

Belinda felt hostility heave and surge in her breast. She had never for a moment expected this, and the girl was doing it deliberately. 'Might I remind you *I* am the guest in this house? As I understand it, you are a Ballinger employee.'

'Oh, my God!' Rosslyn exclaimed, appalled. 'I

haven't heard anything like that for a long time. Please go on. Half my trouble is my sense of the ridiculous.'

Belinda glared back at her with intense dislike. 'You wouldn't dare speak to me like this in front of the family.'

'Exactly. This conversation wouldn't arise. With all humbleness, as a Ballinger employee, which oddly enough the Ballingers have never once mentioned, I'm quite aware of the nature of your visit. You've come to tell me you have high hopes of marrying Boyd and for another woman to look at him is treason. Well, I wish you luck, Miss Russell, in your great venture, but the details of the campaign I don't wish to know. Every word I say, every expression on my face, you just sit and stare at. What does this mean? I'm not blind, Miss Russell, and I'm not stupid either!'

'And neither am I!' Belinda snapped, her eyes glittering. 'It's shockingly plain you're madly in love with him.'

'And you've come here to extinguish the flame?'

'I notice you don't deny it!'

'Would it make any difference if I did? What about you?' Rosslyn put the brush down, plummeted right out of her blissful mood. 'Do *you* love him?'

Belinda's cheeks burned and she let out an infuriated gasp. 'See here, Miss Marshall, my relationship with Boyd and the entire Ballinger family has nothing to do with you.'

'That's a relief!' Rosslyn retorted quite amiably. 'For a minute there I thought I was going to be immersed in it.'

Cold wrath flashed from under Belinda's heavy lids, and she clenched her hands on her knees. 'It just so happens that Boyd and I have had an understanding for years!'

'Lordy!' Rosslyn replied wryly. 'I'd want a man to run after me, not the other way around.'

Belinda jumped to her feet like an opponent who had been hit when she was down. 'How dare you?' She stood over the slighter, smaller Rosslyn like an outraged goddess bent on vengeance.

'I dare, Miss Russell, because I simply don't care. You and your fiery passions don't interest me.'

The cool cutting irony flabbergasted Belinda. As a weapon it couldn't have been more effective. She moved back a few paces and fell once more into the deep, high-backed, chintz-covered armchair. Her face was a study and a fair indication of the strain she was feeling. Rosslyn, angry with herself now, tried to make amends.

'Why don't we start again?' she suggested, not without humour. 'You want me to keep away from Boyd?'

'That's it!' Belinda said with renewed vehemence.

'Well, I'm sorry, but I can't oblige. It would be quite impossible. You must see that. Boyd *is* Belyando, at its highest and deepest level. Up to date I've had a marvellous time. I've seen so much I've never seen before. I've learned a great deal and I've been treated with great courtesy and charm.'

'The Ballingers make these charitable gestures all the time,' Belinda pointed out with cool scorn.

'I'm sure they do, but I'm the first gesture to work with Kylie.'

'That little minx!' At some inner recollection Belinda's eyes flashed. 'She'd have developed along quite another line if I'd had a say in her upbringing.'

'I thought you were a good friend of her mother's?'

'Sonia has done her best!' Belinda retreated with intense irritation. 'Now she's forced to leave it to others. Why you, I don't know. You're simply not responsible enough.'

'Really?' Rosslyn's golden eyes glowed, but she merely shrugged her shoulders. 'If we weren't total strangers or you had the time to give it a little more thought you'd find the reverse is true. I'm over-conscientious. It has been pointed out to me and I believe it. Kylie has a great deal of my sympathy. I'm very fond of her.'

'Oh, spare me!' Belinda threw up a blind hand, wholly uninterested in Kylie. 'It's a wonder you don't feel guilty!' she claimed.

'Of what?'

'Why, of what you're doing, you stupid creature! Boyd loves me!'

'If that were true I might have to adopt another point of view,' Rosslyn replied, adding fuel to the fire. 'Why the devil should he love you?'

'Because I love him.'

Rosslyn sank down on the bed herself, feeling by this time profoundly despondent. 'I'm sorry, Miss Russell, but I don't see that that follows at all, not according to the letters from the lovelorn. One-sided love affairs are happening all the time, which just goes to prove this discussion is both embarrassing and unnecessary. In a few more weeks I go home.'

'I'm hoping for your sake you'll agree to go now.'

'Good heavens!' Rosslyn uttered the words to herself, much struck and rather disgusted by Belinda's warning and cautions. 'There's nowhere else in the world I'd rather be,' she said emphatically.

'Well then!' Belinda stood up and pressed out a non-existent wrinkle in her shocking pink skirt. 'We've no way of knowing how this whole sorry business will turn out. I don't mind telling you Sonia is on my side. She's just as angry and concerned as I am.'

'Mrs. Ballinger can't dictate her brother-in-law's life!'

'She *can* say who should or should not look after her daughter. *I* say you're a bad influence!'

'Fiddlesticks!' Rosslyn looked acutely uncaring.

'And I'm not finished yet. You'll be hearing from Sonia a lot sooner than you expected. We've been friends for years. She introduced me to Boyd. It's highly unlikely she would see her own plans jeopardized.'

'Plans she's unqualified to make.'

Belinda gave way to somewhat contemptuous amusement. 'I tried to make this easy for you, a little friendly advice. Instead of which you choose to cross swords with me – and worse again, Sonia. I find that nauseating and impertinent.'

'Please don't endure my company a moment longer.

May I show you out?'

Belinda rounded on her with surprising malignity, 'That won't be necessary. I suppose it was too much to hope a mere little schoolteacher would have no ambition.'

'Aim high, my father always says,' Rosslyn said calmly, and smiled. 'He's a Supreme Court judge!'

'Well, well! I'm surprised – yes, very surprised.'

'Yes, I could see you thought I was Little Orphan Annie.'

'Then remember what I said!' Belinda burst out violently.

'Of course. Even if it seems particularly unnecessary for you to have said it at all.'

Belinda's polished, well defined face tautened under pressure. She had expected a captive rabbit, instead of which she had got this challenging directness. 'I didn't precipitate this unpleasant episode,' she said bitterly, '*you* did! Believe me, this is no game. I'm deadly serious.'

'I can see that, and it's not your fault. All we can hope for is that the best woman wins!'

'Then I'm home!' Belinda said heatedly, two lines of anger between her jet black shiny brows.

'And all you'd get from me is a cheer. I've a philosophical nature, Miss Russell – tolerant, generous perhaps. It occurs to me that you aren't!'

'Be warned, then!' said Belinda, walking to the door. 'Sonia will have something to add to all this. See if you can laugh *that* off!'

'Actually,' Rosslyn walked after her, 'I'd be very

surprised if she did. Now the barriers are down, surely the smart way to handle these matters is to ignore them?'

'One gets the damnedest people out here!' Belinda gave a short, ugly laugh.

'Don't be so hard on yourself! Now if you'll excuse me I *will* wash my hair. I hate it when I'm not neat.'

'Well, you are decorative in your way. An amusement thing!' Belinda waved her fingers and sauntered off, justly proud of having had the last word.

Oddly enough, that little stinging sally didn't fully affect Rosslyn until half-way through dinner, when she began to burn with a discreet humiliation. It was extremely unkind, not to say spiteful of Belinda, but perhaps there was more than a grain of truth in it. What did she know of Boyd, after all? He had told her in so many ways that he wasn't anxious to commit himself to any woman. Wasn't that enough? She wasn't a huntress like Belinda. It wasn't her nature. She was the nymph that wanted to be pursued and captured. Quite possibly, taking that line, she would lose out. There was strength in Belinda's determination. The sun had come out from behind the clouds and Belinda was at her vivacious best, her mocking ill humour quite vanished, gossiping, gossiping, gossiping, her conversation richly sprinkled with names Rosslyn had never even heard of, but then Belinda wasn't that willing to let bygones be bygones.

Ellie for once was letting the team down, sitting with great calmness and unfashionable splendour, locked in a thought-crowded silence of her own. Usually Belinda's singularly exaggerated statements irritated her no end, but now she was not only willing to overlook them, she never even heard them. Ellie had something on her mind, Rosslyn was certain of it. She could hardly stay at the table herself, toying with an excellent dinner and drinking rather more of the brilliant Barossa Valley dry red than was good for her. She was, in fact, no drinker at all, and even now her neck felt funny.

But she did look beautiful, which was why Belinda was talking so vivaciously, challenging every eye, defying them to look across the table at Rosslyn, who looked like a whole roomful of yellow roses. Her long, bare-topped dress was just a filmy drift of sun yellow sheer voile. It was inexpensive but very cool and pretty, and her glorious colour turned it into something Kylie called 'quite smashing'. Belinda's embossed white satin pyjamas which had cost the earth didn't have anywhere near the same magical effect, and Belinda decided there and then that though she had the rare figure for slacks she would stick to long dresses for evening wear for the rest of her visit.

If Boyd shot the odd, sharp glance at her during the course of the dinner, Rosslyn missed it, being sunk in a wordless mood of melancholia and a wine-induced insensitivity to her surroundings. She looked for all the world like the lovely picture Derek was promising his public. Her eyes, golden and faintly tilted, were deeply feminine in her face, innocently alluring, full of secrets, when she was thinking very little at all by this time. Her head was quite muzzy. Strong black coffee might fix it.

She never had more than one glass every other night.

Somehow she found herself away from the formal ambiance of the dining-room and out in the wide, spacious entrance hall, where Kylie startled her with a fevered, time-honoured:

'Psst!'

'What is it?'

Kylie didn't answer but jerked back her head to indicate of all places Ellie's private retreat and sitting-room.

'You're the first, outside Ellie, that is.'

'That's refreshing! I hope it's not a pet skink!'

'Skinks actually make good pets. There are six hundred species of them, you know. Most of them are under a foot. They're very retiring but devoted. I had a blue-tongue once, but I fed it too many snails and slugs and it died. They twist their tails off like the geckos to get away from their enemies.'

'Yes, I know. Listen, sweetie, I'm in a pretty wild state myself. What is it?'

'Come along and see!' Kylie invited, with a grand sweep of her arm, ushering Rosslyn into Ellie's den and quietly slamming the door.

'Good grief!'

'I'm pretty happy about it!' Kylie announced radiantly in the background.

'So this is what you and Ellie have been up to. Well done. *Well done.* Oh, Kylie!' Rosslyn moved backwards and caught the child about the waist to give her a quick congratulatory kiss on her fully prepared cheek. 'If I hadn't had one drink too many I would have to toast you again.'

There was an affectionate pause as they both looked towards an extraordinary and extensive collection of Kylie's most significant drawings executed in acrylic paint on cardboard. It was all very wildly intense and nationalistic, the results of a powerful and very personal experience, a brilliant and imaginative child's vision of the landscape around her. It was tropical North Queensland, the weirdly beautiful and rather threatening atmosphere of the rain forest, one of the last great reserves of nature, with its soaring trees and heavy buttresses, the thick ropes of lawyer vines, the interlacing lianas, birds and animals and reptiles and assorted mythical beasts, peering out of the tall spiky grasslands, or sheltering under the giant forest ferns, cassowarys and tree kangaroos making spectacular daring leaps from tree to tree where unbelievably brilliant birds flashed: virulent green pythons that would make one's hair stand up on end and an astonishingly accurate drawing of an orchid, superb for a child going on nine, a dendrobium, a very beautiful and exotic tropical orchid, with large, pendulous many-flowered racemes; not an orchid that could be cut and taken into the house but incomparably beautiful growing, as Rosslyn had seen it, in its natural habitat the warm humid conditions of the monsoonal rain forests. It was ivory, pink-tinged at the edges, with a golden-centred bulb and large, elliptic, freshly green leaves.

'Marvellous!' Rosslyn breathed. 'Every single creative impulse chanelled into constructive action, and we have Ellie to thank for it, bless her! They're superb!'

'Yes, aren't they!' Kylie seconded fondly, inspired by Rosslyn's sincere ardour.

'You're a genuine primitive!'

'That's what I thought myself!'

'And such a notable collection!'

'Mostly the rain forest, as you can see. We picked the orchid – Ellie got a blister from it. It died, of course, but I worked pretty fast. Ellie said I'm remarkably accomplished, 'specially considering I'm mostly self-taught!'

'And your first one-woman show!' Rosslyn enthused in turn. 'Are you going to call in the others?'

'No way!' The suggestion threw Kylie into an artistic ferment. 'Only Uncle Boyd. I'll slip out and get him.'

'But, darling, one must have an audience.'

'Yes, but I don't want anyone around here patronizing me. Or us, Ellie and me. She's my agent.'

'All artists need patrons, Kylie. I'm sure all this will be very much admired.'

'No. Only you and Uncle Boyd.' Kylie indicated her point-blank refusal for a mass showing. 'Daddy would only think they're bits of a crazy jigsaw puzzle.'

'Why don't you ask him?' Rosslyn suggested quietly. 'You might be in for a very pleasant surprise!'

'Daddy doesn't give away prizes!' Kylie sheered away violently. 'If I have to pick one of them, I'll settle for Mother. She's been rather nice lately!'

'Well, let the thought simmer!' Rosslyn herself

moved away, circling the room, giving each painting her full critical attention. They were so good, or so it seemed to her, she felt vaguely like crying, so she coughed instead. Kylie was equally pleased, divining Rosslyn's true feelings and feeling like shedding a few tears herself, like a new mother with her most cherished possession. Her collection. It was all very violent and dynamic, the picturesque fauna and flora, the riotous freedom of self-expression, and Kylie stood there in her blue-flowered nightie and brunch coat, very much the talented and intense artist, who would be eagerly sought in the years to come, or so Ellie had said.

Rosslyn, her head slightly reeling, came to the end of this brilliant and prolific display. Some of the paintings were quite claustrophobic, conveying a locked-in feeling such as she had experienced herself in the heavily vaulted rain jungle. If one parted all that seething mass of green! . . . It was tropical nature with abundant life everywhere, even under a torn-off strip of bark. Kylie's work would always have just that touch of the macabre, a preoccupation with inner experiences applied to nature. Even as a child she was curiously distinctive, and a shade disquietening as all true virtuosos are. When a quick rap on the door came, both girls whirled around, looking positively threatened.

Belinda, her cheeks glowing and her eyes jetty black with excitement, stood on the threshold in her gleaming white satin pyjama suit, looking entirely untrustworthy. 'Now what are you two up to?'

Without a word, Kylie slipped her cold little hand into Rosslyn's, and Rosslyn tightened her grip on the little girl. Together they faced a common adversary, Belinda, with her avid, glamorous, dangerous face. 'It's your business, I suppose?' Rosslyn demanded, thinking she had best meet fire with fire seeing her own position was precisely defined – protector to Kylie.

Belinda's hostile, curious gaze shifted, became transfixed. The colour died out of her cheeks, leaving them rather sallow.

'I can't believe it!' she said, a strange expression flitting across her face. 'Really, this child needs a good psycho-analyst!'

'It's all part of being brilliant!' Rosslyn maintained.

Kylie flushed scarlet and bit her lip hard. 'Can you draw yourself?' she demanded suddenly of Belinda.

'No, I can't!' Belinda said stiffly, eyeing the child with active dislike in her eyes.

'Well then, what would *you* know?' Kylie flashed back with nearly adult satire.

'Kylie!' Rosslyn remonstrated with a nervous clench on Kylie's rigid little hand.

Belinda was nearly beside herself, not only with Kylie's impertinence. 'What kind of terrible dreams does this child have?'

'Dreams?' Rosslyn asked mockingly.

'Nightmares, if you like! They're not exactly joyous, are they?'

'I think they're excellent!' Rosslyn said, sharply pressing Kylie's stiffening hand.

'God, they're not even Derek!' Belinda exploded, continuing to gaze wide-eyed at Kylie's ferocious, primitive, pagan energies. 'I don't think this place is good for the child!'

'Shows what you know!' Kylie interrupted very rudely indeed.

'I'll call the others,' said Belinda, making it sound like a threat, which in its way it was. She went rapidly to the open doorway, calling out a perfectly evil and intensely jarring: 'Yoo-hoo! We're in Ellie's room!'

Kylie trembled violently, making a silent vow to herself not to overlook Belinda's calculated piece of treachery. Thus directed, the rest of the family were converging upon them, a grand muster, moving as a single unit into the room, Boyd and Ellie first with acute observation and little change of expression; Sonia, all pleasant and surprised attention; Derek, in his somewhat moony fashion at his wife's back, until his eye fell upon Kylie's extraordinary body of work. Then he came to a halt, looking for all the world as if his most cherished hopes were about to perish.

'What in the world—?' he asked with every appearance of shock.

'My dearest baby, yours?' Sonia gasped, running lightly forward, craning her elegant blonde head, looking for a signature as a point of reference.

'Mine!' Kylie admitted with great deliberation, beginning to scowl blackly.

'Well, it adds up to all those hours you've had to yourself!' Boyd Ballinger murmured, briskly circling the room, something of an art connoisseur himself. 'Sooner or later, Miss Kylie Ballinger, you're going to make quite a name for yourself.'

'Do you like them, Uncle Boyd?' Kylie asked in a tight little voice that betrayed her inner torment.

'To be frank, darling, I'm quite stunned. I can see we're all going to have to take you very seriously indeed. Well, Derek, what do you say?' He turned his dark head and gave his stepbrother a hard speaking glance. 'How come we haven't had a comment?'

'It isn't easy!' Derek Ballinger muttered quite grimly.

'Poor child!' Belinda directed her pitying gaze away from Kylie to Boyd's chiselled, deeply intent profile. 'You can't be serious, Boyd?'

'But really these are extremely good, don't you think, Belinda? There's raw material here for years to come. That orchid is incredible for such a young artist – the observation and the detail. My own Belyando seen through the eyes of a gifted child. It's all a little lavish and heady, with a very colourful imagination but such vitality! It's consistent with Kylie.'

Ellie suddenly gave a great shout of triumph. 'There, what did I tell you?' she demanded of no one in particular.

'You always were avant-garde, Ellie!' Derek Ballinger said.

'And I've always been proven right!' Ellie pointed out bracingly from the depths of her truly individual nature. She turned and smiled very benignly on Rosslyn and Kylie, who were still holding hands like babes in the wood, fused to one another for support.

'I didn't want anyone to see them, and they wouldn't have but for *her*!' Kylie burst out wrathfully, writing under her father's seemingly outraged silence, her blue eyes glittering over Belinda's tall, equally scornful figure.

'Why not even your own mama?' Sonia very nearly wailed, hurt by Kylie's trenchant and revealing comment.

'Well, yes, I was going to ask you, Mama,' said Kylie, struggling briefly with a white lie, but there were tears in her mother's eyes, real tears, and they began to lick at Kylie like a flame. A turbulent little creature she might have been, but she was very tender-hearted.

She let go of Rosslyn's hand and ran over to her mother, who encircled her daughter's small figure with one slender protective arm, turning to demand of her closest girl friend:

'How is it, Belinda, you can't see how very good these drawings are?'

'They're too curious for me, dear!' Belinda said tightly, intensely irritated by the proud maternal gleam in Sonia's pale blue eyes.

'And when are we going to hear from you, little one?' Boyd Ballinger moved quietly towards Rosslyn, his voice low and surely caressing, turning her heart over. She tilted her head towards him, listening to his voice, but not ready to answer him yet. He gave a brief laugh and unexpectedly reached out a hand to tug at her bright, silky curls. 'Well, *really*, Rosslyn! You just stand there looking unbelievably beautiful and dreamy with not one word to say for yourself, the entire evening, practically struck dumb.'

'That always seems to happen when I drink wine!'

she explained softly.

'There's little doubt about that to my mind. Later on I'll take you out for a breath of fresh air, but first, what of Kylie?'

'Why, I've always felt the same way about Kylie. However do you think I became her champion?'

'Not because her name is Ballinger.' It was no question but a quiet statement and he lifted a finger and inched back a silky tendril that had drifted out on to her cheek. 'Do you know, Rosslyn, if I didn't have such a wise head on my shoulders, I'd very probably fall in love with you. As it is, it's very difficult not to make love to you.'

'And Belinda?' she barely whispered, her golden eyes challenging him.

'What do you want me to do about her?'

'I honestly don't know!' she said frankly.

'What's the connection anyway?'

'Heavens, why ask me? I don't understand you at all.'

'Too bad! But I can make you tremble, which is better than nothing.'

His taunting eyes touched on her face and throat and she felt the quick heat prickle her skin. 'I'm as susceptible as the next woman,' she said sweetly. 'I have to admit you dazzle me. You *do*, but don't underestimate me.'

'Why, you cheeky little beggar! Why should I damned well do that?'

'Oh, I don't know!' She looked up at him with soft desolation and he took a deep breath, a curious expression on his hard, handsome face.

'You know, Rosslyn,' he said, and his voice sprang the leash of a tight self-control, 'this whole situation is getting right out of hand.'

'Do you want me to go? Belinda suggested I might.'

'On the contrary,' he said curtly, 'I don't think I can afford to let you go at all.'

'That's madness!'

'Yes, isn't it?' He moved away from her indolently back to the main group.

Belinda, her eyes shadowed, fuming and fretting inside, turned on Derek with uncontrolled impatience. 'For God's sake, Derek, how long do we have to wait for your enlightened opinion? Frankly, I'm bored!'

'*And* uncommonly irritable!' Derek said in his soft, dry fashion. 'Well, Belinda darling, it's all very nice. Not exactly what I would have done myself as a child.'

'Then don't be misled because of it,' Boyd said, and his voice had a hard note of reproof in it.

At once Derek flushed and he turned on his stepbrother with quick anger. 'God, Boyd, you sound like the old man sometimes – arrogant as the very devil!'

'Don't be such a damned fool! Can't you see what you're doing to Kylie? Your opinion is very important to her, yet you seem to be withholding it.'

'Not at all. Not at all!' Derek defended himself. 'It's just there's not much I *can* say! The last thing I want to do is discourage my own daughter – after all, what talent she has springs from me, but these are obviously just childish flights of fancy!'

The peculiar cruelty of this struck Rosslyn violently. She fired right up to the roots of her hair. 'It seems to me, Mr. Ballinger,' she burst out wrathfully, 'you'll never be able to withdraw that statement. How a man of your gifts should be so blind I don't know, but that's not the worst part! Kylie is your daughter. Surely she's entitled to a most sympathetic reception, not an adult judgment delivered with a ferocious lack of insight and tact? *I* don't want to sit for you any more, anyway!'

'Hear, hear, child!' shouted Ellie, her eyes alighting on Rosslyn as though she found her splendid. 'Derek may be startled in the extreme, but I think he deserves it. Take heed, boy, as a warning!'

Everyone seemed to be watching Rosslyn with varying degrees of condemnation and pardon. Belinda, hard, flat and narrow and a plain how-dare-you! Sonia and Kylie white-faced and grave, Ellie blazing steadily with thoughts of her own, Derek ashen, like a man under attack. Rosslyn dared not look at Boyd. All that suggested itself to her was flight. She was astonished at herself anyway. She picked up the skirt of her long yellow dress and ran from the room, dazzled by the brilliance of the big chandelier in the hall. She dashed out into the jasmine-scented night air, breathing it in, trying to control herself. She had spoken out and now there was an immeasurable chasm between herself and the Ballingers. But she didn't care. She had sacrificed herself for Kylie. That was what friends were for. One simply had to have loyalty.

The night air slipped over her body like silk. What

was she doing out here in the dark? Such precarious moments only happened to other people, not her. Belyando, one way and another, had effected a shattering upheaval in her otherwise uneventful life. Tonight she had properly burned her boats and the consequences were soon to follow. She had spoken out from the heart, but probably her behaviour was a bit immature.

It didn't seem possible that Derek Ballinger was blind to the merits of his daughter's efforts, yet it was a curious fact that even great artists had been ridiculed and disparaged by their equally gifted contemporaries. Inspiration sprang from so many experiences and sources, so many points of view, so many different ideas and preoccupations, but did he have to be so brutally frank when he spent a good deal of his time decrying his own father's attitude towards all his own early artistic manifestations? Perhaps Derek Ballinger had more of his father in him than he cared to think about. Tonight he had given every appearance of being totally insensitive to the feelings of his own little daughter. It was unforgivable, and Rosslyn didn't feel he was entitled to any belated apology from her.

As for Belinda, underneath that glossy exterior was pure dross. At least Sonia was thawing out nicely, realizing perhaps that if she failed to act now in her daughter's best interests, the next opportunity might come too late. Even the worst mothers seemed to have that inbuilt faculty. Probably they were all talking it out now and deciding what to do with Rosslyn. Her days at Belyando had run out, she could be sure of that, and following on this catastrophic twist of fate she had better go indoors and pack. She was ready to leave in any case. She hadn't the courage to wait around for an engagement announcement. The nicest men in the world were horribly cruel. They took no great pleasure from it, it was just part of being a male, with a perpetual deep gulf between the sexes. What a man disregarded entirely could be nectar itself to a woman.

The white-latticed pagoda shimmered before her, smothered in jasmine and the closed cerise trumpets of the morning glories. Suddenly her eyes filled with tears. The things that one looked forward to with great joy so often came to nothing. She should never have fallen in love with Boyd. It had seemed ordained, but now it would take a very long time to straighten herself out again. The only person she had any real control over was herself. It was a hard lesson, the worst one really, to fall in love and not be loved in return. And of course, she wanted marriage from the man she loved, a secure and permanent relationship when there was no real security anywhere. One could only live a day at a time. With her nature and training anything less than marriage was unthinkable, yet she could see the funny side of it. Marriage, the great settlement, the dizzying pinnacle of a girl's career, the seal on her desirability. Boyd didn't want marriage. No woman was *that* supremely necessary to his wellbeing. He needed no other direction in life. He had Belyando, the very breath of life.

There were all sorts of funny ghostly noises in the tropical night. Even the garden seemed bathed in an unreal light like a perfumed jungle full of enchanted

snakes. A fruit bat screeched overhead, diving in ec-
stasy into the golden, fruit-laden branches of the giant
mango trees. Rosslyn lifted her head, staring at its tiny
inky black shadow against the moon, trembling violently when lean hands grasped her firmly from behind
locking her delicate shoulders into a hard grip. She had
no need to turn her head to know it was Boyd.

'The life you've stirred up around here!' he said, and
gave a low, hard laugh.

'Oh, I'm sorry about all that,' she began in a tor-
mented fashion as though she had come out into the
garden to languish or drown in the lagoon.

'Why?' He swung her round towards him in his
vivid, vital way. 'You gave every appearance of having
a wonderful time. Derek is stunned, knocked breathless
by a few words of criticism. He happens to be a famous
man, in case you've forgotten.'

'Well, he's far from being his daughter's best friend!'
Rosslyn burst out recklessly, trying to wriggle out from
under his hard, pinning hands.

'Stop that!' he gritted, very hard. 'If I hurt you you
wouldn't like it. Be that as it may, he's not used to being
ticked off in company. It seems to me, Rosslyn, I've
committed my own kind of folly in always looking at
you through rose-coloured glasses.'

'And now I'm very much in the way?'

'Well, inside anyway!' he agreed with a soft, sardonic laugh. 'With reason! The curious part is, Derek in
his own way is every bit as intolerant as my father was.
Sonia and Belinda are now very politely at one
another's throats. Ellie is egging them on, very much in

her element, at the same time removing a goggle-eyed Kylie from the scene. The enormity of it all!'

'And Derek?'

'Derek has retired to his studio, the only congenial place in the house. You may apologize in the morning.'

'I'm not going to,' she said, firming her chin.

'Oh yes, you are! I for one want to see the finished portrait.'

'Why not commission one of Belinda instead?'

'What for?'

'Oh, why don't you be honest?' she cried in a temper, oblivious to the sudden tautness that was etched on his face.

'All in due time.'

He was holding her rather cruelly intent, but she didn't even notice it, her golden eyes glowing, accusing him: 'You don't give a damn how much you make other people suffer, do you?'

'Women, you mean?'

'Belinda!' she qualified, and her voice broke, betraying her.

'My sweet little idiot, you appear to have your mind perfectly made up about Belinda, yet I'm out here with you in the moonlight.'

'What for?' she challenged him.

'Right now, I can't imagine!' Some elemental antagonism began to prowl in his eyes and she lifted her head defiantly.

'It will take me about an hour to pack.'

'No, thank you, little one!' he drawled. 'Don't

bother me with nonsense.'

'Oh well, I did offer!' Rosslyn clamped her teeth shut with controlled hysteria, lifting her face to the night wind. 'I love Belyando, but I know now I should never have come here.'

'Yes indeed!' Boyd said dryly, his glittery gaze on her upturned face and her throat and her bare shoulders. 'But there have been some rewards, surely?'

'You?'

'Why not?'

'You only think you know me!' she warned him, passionate rebellion and a flare of pride starting way down deep inside her. Somehow she would have to find the strength to get away from him.

His mouth twisted ironically. 'Then tell me about the real you. Not the funny, sweet, sad, occasionally fiery little brat I see before me, but so beautiful, damn you!' He pulled her into his arms and held her still, his fingers tracing the curve of her neck and closing over her collarbone while her eyes clung to his in a kind of mesmerization. Her body began responding for her, engulfed in fire, yielding to the insistent caressing hands.

'Kiss me and I'll scream!' she said in a perverse rush.

'How come you're whispering?' His laugh was low and derisive. 'This is no dreadful dream, flower face, this is real, and I *am* going to kiss you. I can't think how I've held out so long!'

She averted her head and set her small white teeth with a determination of her own, cherishing the fact that she was showing positive physical proof that she still had some vestige of pride left, but it was only a brief burst of decision, for his hand cupped her chin, exerting just a little pressure on either side of her face so that the line of her mouth altered and became tremulous and parted. The tension went out of her and all that was left was an intense abandonment to the moment. She would always have that.

The night wind filled her ears, rushing and roaring, the stars seemed to plunge for her scattering sparks, and Boyd lowered his head, kissing her just as she knew it would be. She clung to him with a fatal headlong reaction, the only person in the whole wide world who really mattered, alone in the fragrant eternal moonlight and magic. She had forfeited her pride and her armour – everything. It wasn't only desire that was flooding through her, but love, surging to each sensitive nerve end. It was not possible he didn't know this golden flame for what it was.

'Boyd?' She felt absolutely shattered, trailing her soft mouth against the tantalizing smooth roughness of his chin, the deeply moulded cleft.

'Talk to me tomorrow!' he said with a faint laugh in his voice.

She tried to appeal to him once more, but he was kissing her again with a slow, brilliant expertise that made words seem meaningless. Her small shining head was thrown back against the hard curve of his shoulder and when he finally let her go tears started behind her tightly closed eyelids.

'Don't cry,' he whispered.

'I'm not.'

'Well, open your eyes, then.' His hand dropped to her nape, exquisitely gentle. 'What am I going to do with you, Rosslyn? We can't keep meeting like this. Or *I* can't!'

Her beautiful eyes were shimmering, staring into his dark, mocking face. 'Always you laugh,' she said. 'You've been laughing at me since the moment we met.'

'What would you have me do?' he asked, arrogance and something else in his strongly sculptured face. 'You know damned well I have to recognize a few of the conventions.'

'Out here?' she said rashly, her heart storming.

'Rosslyn, my lamb, I *know* you. You're a doe-eyed innocent, and I'm going to take you back to the house before my protective instincts run out.'

'You don't need to!' She broke away from him, breathless. 'Is this what you do when a relationship reaches a certain level? Back off? I think that's decidedly odd.'

He reached out a hand and brushed her silky soft curls. 'Don't go all emotional on me.'

'Why, are you afraid of emotion?'

His soft laugh brushed her cheek. 'Is that what you really think?'

'I don't know,' she said, desperately afraid of her own revealed needs. 'You're quite incredible. Do you kiss everyone like you kiss me?'

'For what it's worth, *no*!' He smiled at her, his teeth very white in his dark face, his voice almost casual, laced with self-mockery. 'I was forewarned about you, Rosslyn, so I've only myself to blame. On the other hand, I don't feel I can rush you into marriage at the earliest opportunity.'

'Oh!' She shied away from all his splendid dark arrogance, almost as though he had struck her.

'Well, you did ask for it, baby girl. It's not easy to commit oneself totally to another human being.'

'Surely one doesn't have to *learn* how to love?' she asked almost tragically, her mouth still throbbing with a sweet burning fierceness, the touch and the scent of him. It clung to her.

'And you love me?'

So hard and imperious was the inflection in his voice, her heart lunged with shock. She swung her head sharply to stare up at him. With the moon at the back of him, raying over his left shoulder, he looked very tall and oddly untameable, capable of anything. Certainly not good husband material, with brilliant sardonic humour in his blue-green eyes, too vividly masculine. Her own melancholy, bitter-sweet expression flared into one of open defiance, her lovely face touched with excitement and an unaccustomed hostility.

'*No!*' she said fiercely. 'No. No. A thousand times *no*! You're a hurtful, hateful man. You're a devil!'

It was the lick of flame towards dynamite. Without even seeming to move he had both of her wrists pinned in one steely lock. 'Who's afraid now?' he demanded with terrifying quiet.

Rosslyn was dazed, melting at his touch despite herself.

'Do you know just how big Belyando is? We could vanish in a night. Do you want to come? Answer me! Now's as good a time as ever!'

'You're hurting me!'

'Now that you mention it, I like it! Well, you precious little idiot, you delicious, delightful, endearing, devastating little witch! You're the one who's arousing all these crazy notions.'

'You're doing this deliberately.'

'Of course I am,' he said, watching her like a hawk. 'You said you loved me. Prove it.'

'I've no clear recollection of saying anything of the kind!' she said, wildly unsettled.

'And you talk about lessons and loving!' he said, in a hard, stinging tone.

'I wouldn't go anywhere with you,' she said in a choked little voice, trying to hurt him as he was hurting her.

'And you won't have any say in it!' He swung her right up into his arms, his manner downright hostile, and she experienced a powerful rush of fright. Boyd in this mood was positively dangerous. Her hands linked themselves around his neck and she could feel herself shaking. She turned her face into his cheek with a blinding wave of love that shook him almost as much as it shook her.

'Rosslyn?' The arrogance had left his voice and the irony. 'I should be able to resist you, but I can't!'

Her hand travelled down the brown column of his neck and she turned up her mouth, all in the space of a few seconds willing to go anywhere with him. 'Kiss me,

Boyd. I want you to.'

'And you think I don't know that!' he said, holding her implacably. 'If I do you won't get away from me.'

'And I think I actually want you that badly. It's so odd and unexpected and rather frightening, and it's never happened to me before.'

'And it's not even going to happen to you now. A minute ago I was never going to let you go; now I feel I have to. It occurs to me I should, or could, love you. Why else would I be putting you down?'

'Could it be Belinda's coming?' she said very shortly.

'Don't try to be smart! Is she?'

'Look around.'

Belinda was at this point speedily crossing the grass.

'Reinforcements!' Rosslyn said, rather bitterly for her.

'Easy!' His hand closed over her shoulder, steadying her much as though she were a runaway filly.

'Boy ... y ... yd!' Belinda was calling, obviously having a hard time of it finding them.

'Go on, answer her!' Rosslyn invited.

'What would you suggest? Name, rank, serial number, that kind of thing?'

'What about, "here, darling!"'

'It occurs to me, Rosslyn, that you're jealous.'

'Keep your exalted opinions for Belinda!' she cried, instinctively reacting and starting to run away.

'All right!' he said simply, with no visible sign of anger. 'Make your escape, you silly little ostrich. I can't fail to catch up with you the next day.'

161

CHAPTER SEVEN

THE next day, Rosslyn found herself apologizing to Derek. It presented no great problem, for Derek was one of those people whose art blocked them off from all the grimmer aspects of life. He shrugged off Rosslyn's few half-hearted, heart-thumping words and requested her immediate presence in the studio. There still remained a few technical problems he had to overcome and he was adamant about working that morning, so much so that Rosslyn, after a bad, dream-freighted night, felt it her duty, more or less, to fall into line. All of the Ballingers in their own way were dictators, but Derek lacked Boyd's irresistible charm.

Her wide tilted eyes were shadowed this morning. All she really wanted to do was get in the jeep and drive endlessly, endlessly, with the wind in her hair and the deeply blue, storm-washed sky above her, for the early hours had been punctuated with heavy downpours that miraculously cleared before dawn. Every bit of her composure seemed to have deserted her. She had scarcely been able to choke down a morsel of toast and the hand that held her coffee cup visibly trembled. At least in the light-filled studio she could relax. She didn't have to outwit or outmanoeuvre Derek. She didn't even have to engage him in conversation.

His lean Ballinger face was enormously grave, overwhelmed with preoccupation, his right hand sweeping over the canvas with great fluency, his glance never wavering when it was fixed on his model or the painted image he was creating. He was content. It was all working out extremely well, and Sonia's exquisite honey-gold chiffon evening dress, pinned from behind to a perfect fit, was precisely what he wanted. Trust Sonia to come up with this, for Rosslyn simply did not possess anything he considered suitable. This would be one of his flaming achievements. It didn't matter if he was not altogether in favour of his model as a real person. She had too much to say for herself, for one thing, but her colouring and her physical beauty he cherished with all his heart. He felt entirely confident he was transferring it to canvas to be lovingly preserved as a Derek Ballinger masterpiece. He had even allowed Sonia a brief glance at the unfinished portrait last evening and she had nearly fainted away at its brilliance and promise. Dear Sonia! She had always understood him.

The young girl in the portrait was very beautiful – in love, illuminated. Now how could that be? Boyd, of course. Boyd always was singled out by women. A dark, splendid devil, the cattle baron. The old man had been fairly irresistible too. Almost for a moment Derek could have curled up with envy, then he turned his unwinking blue gaze back on the slender delicacy of the girl's form. There was no repose in her today, and her face had lost its tender, dreaming expression. Faint shadows lay under her golden eyes, some trace of passion? She was certainly capable of it, a union of those eyes and that mouth. That vision kept his artistic spirit excited for a full thirty minutes, while Rosslyn was nearly fainting, not able to sustain the ecstatic immobility Derek required. Her satiny cream and rose-tinted flesh was subdued to a pallor today. She craved a brief interval of rest, but Derek's concentration was absolute, the unique temperament of the true artist. He was a perfectionist as he had been all his life and now he was possessed with the intricate drapery of the chiffon.

Rosslyn almost but not quite pulled a face at him. She felt not a little distraught, as if something bad was about to happen.

'I know you're hot and uncomfortable in that long gown,' Derek surprised her by saying, 'but in just a few minutes I'll be finished with you. The results will outweigh all your discomforts, you'll see. You have my favourite colouring, do you know that? Delicate but very exact features, and your almond-shaped eyes are just the bizarre touch I like. This is no slick piece of portraiture. It's one of the best things I've done.'

I'll believe it when I see it! Rosslyn thought to herself, blinking her 'almond eyes' rapidly. She was beginning to feel like a marble statue with all her muscles locked and useless.

There was a loud knock on the door that neither of them had the opportunity to answer, for Ellie threw back the door to demand in a sharp, authoritative voice:

'Where's Kylie?'

'She's not here!' Derek replied, possessed of a sudden

ennui. Derek was one of the few people not to make any concessions to Ellie's status in the house, as Ellie refused to make any concessions to Derek's fame.

'Is she nowhere around?' Rosslyn asked quickly, detecting strain beneath Ellie's briskness.

'I've looked everywhere,' said Ellie, sounding as though they might never hear from Kylie again.

'Surely she wouldn't go off without telling you?'

'After last night!' Ellie cried, turning in seconds from a handsome and daunting elderly lady to a frail, unfamiliar figure consumed with hidden tears.

'Oh, Ellie, you know very well Kylie will turn up again. You're putting yourself through needless worry. Look, I'll go for her. She's probably at one of our favourite haunts.'

'You don't give a damn, do you?' Ellie hiccoughed back a tear, glaring at Derek. 'If Kylie's missing we have you to thank!'

'Oh, *please*!' Derek said with weary disinterest. 'Isn't it enough that you've enlisted Rosslyn's help? Kylie has only escaped the monotony of the house. She'll turn up when she's good and ready, so spare me!'

Ellie turned up her hands in a gesture of prayer. 'I'm worried!' she said again, her unseeing gaze on some imagined catastrophe. 'Kylie might look the whole world over and not find another father like you!'

'I'd better go now!' Rosslyn announced with decision. Already she was pulling pins from the hidden back zip. The beautiful gown hung rather precariously and she stepped behind the carved Indian screen, changing into her lettuce green jersey tee-shirt and her cotton drill slacks. A striped silk scarf went with it and she knotted it around her hair, aware of the tension and the ill feeling in the room behind her.

'Isn't this a bit drastic?' Derek was asking, quite genuinely bewildered by the turn of events. Ellie always did make him feel a small boy. 'Nothing ever goes wrong with Kylie!'

Both women ignored him, their slight good will evaporating, as they moved of one accord to the door. Derek only hesitated a minute, then he slammed the door after them. Outside in the corridor, Ellie's tall spare figure suddenly shook with sobs.

'It's incredible for me to break down like this, but I know in my bones something is wrong. Perhaps the child feels her father has betrayed her!'

'Did she say so?'

'She didn't say anything!' Ellie volunteered tonelessly. 'I waited for a tirade, a tantrum, but nothing happened. She just went quietly to bed.'

'She was asleep when I called in,' said Rosslyn. 'Not feigning sleep, really asleep. I checked. Kylie has a good head on her shoulders. She's more like Boyd than Derek.'

'Thank God!' Ellie said piously. 'Yet who knows what she might do?' The chill inside her was invading her voice.

'Where's Sonia?' Rosslyn asked.

'Swallowing tea with Belinda.'

'You have to tell her.'

'What? And have a squawking nerve case on my

hands!'

'Ellie dear!' Rosslyn said patiently, 'we have to tell Sonia and take our chances. She's Kylie's mother. She *must* be told. Could you get hold of the jeep for me? One of the boys will bring it up. Where's Boyd?'

'He'll be gone for hours. Last night caused a flash flood in some of the watering places. Will you tell Sonia? You might be able to manage it with less fuss. I mean, she's bad enough, but *him*!' Fright and anxiety had caused Ellie to lose all her tact and reticence. She went off ranting to herself, reduced by her anxious love for a child to a shadow of herself, beyond all pretence and restraint. 'Please God, let her be all right!'

In the sun-dappled shade of the courtyard, Sonia took the news every bit as badly as Ellie had predicted. She raised her slender white arms to heaven, reacting very strongly.

'It's incredible! My baby's gone. I had no idea! My dear baby, sneaking away on her own! I *never* suspected!'

'Oh, hang on, Sonia,' Belinda said smugly. 'Kylie's a lot smarter than we like to give her credit for.'

Sonia looked anything but grateful for this piece of information. 'That's very generous of you, Belle, but actually I've always thought my daughter brilliant!'

'Oh, I'm sorry, I didn't know!' said Belinda, looking at Rosslyn with accelerating dislike.

Rosslyn glanced away from her quickly and smiled at Sonia. 'I don't think there's any real need to worry, Mrs. Ballinger. Kylie's very likely at one of our usual haunts. I'll go and check now.'

Sonia, however, was consumed with panic, ready to tear her long blonde hair out. 'It's a judgment!' she announced.

Belinda was embarrassed. Sonia had never adhered to any strong religious beliefs, yet now she was wringing her hands and calling on heaven. 'Settle down, Sonia!' she said gruffly. 'It's not like you to give way!' She obviously meant well, but it came out in a singularly clumsy way.

Sonia ignored her. 'I haven't taken my duty as a mother half seriously enough. Now perhaps I'm about to be punished. Does Derek know?'

'He sees no cause to panic, Mrs. Ballinger.'

'He wouldn't!' Sonia returned bitterly. 'He's like that! Sometimes his behaviour is a total mystery to me. He's devoted his whole life to his work. Even I come second best, and I could have married anyone. Yes, *anyone*!'

'You could too,' Belinda soothed, by way of solace.

'I'd like to go now, Mrs. Ballinger,' said Rosslyn, feeling she was wasting valuable time.

'I'll come with you!' Sonia said, erupting into instant activity.

'Better still, can't we take the jeep? You and I, Sonia. I can't see that you need bother at all, Miss Marshall,' said Belinda, alerted to the extraordinary misalliance between her friend and the redheaded schoolteacher.

'Well, actually, I think she's being most wonderfully kind!' Sonia retorted. 'However, there is no substitute for a mother's love or a mother's presence.'

'Then take the jeep!' Rosslyn suggested. 'You may be able to find Boyd a whole lot quicker than I would. He'll know what to do, but very likely we're worrying needlessly. Children are very unpredictable. Especially Kylie. She could be indulging a fit of temperament some place.'

'If only that's true!' Sonia cried, seeing a grain of truth in this assertion. 'One never realizes how much one loves one's children until things of this kind happen. In some ways, Kylie has had a rotten childhood. *I* had one, now that I come to think of it. My parents spent most of their time in England. Yes, I'm a good deal to blame. The lessons one learns through life! I can see I'm upsetting you, Rosslyn. I'm sorry. As a teacher, you must hear this all the time. I want to say now how much I appreciate all you've done for Kylie. I can't think why I haven't mentioned it before. You've worked wonders, really. Kylie is all the better for your companionship and guidance.'

Belinda was making scornful noises, irritated and amazed that Rosslyn was about to be initiated into the privileged ranks of one of Sonia's friends. 'Well, let's go, dear!' she said with her first act of diplomacy. 'We can hold a conference on the run!'

'And to think I thought this break was going to be idyllic!' Sonia went off moaning.

Left to herself, Rosslyn gave herself no time to reconsider. She would certainly go looking herself. She had only her intuition to go on, but she thought she could find Kylie quicker than anyone. Sonia and Belinda had taken Boyd's route, she would stick to the haunts Kylie seemed to favour. She had a deep unwillingness to venture too far into the bush, but she didn't think that would be necessary. A few minutes later she finished girthing up Lucy, the little chestnut mare, and hauled herself into the saddle knowing a brief burst of achievement at her increasing prowess. She touched the reins lightly and the compact little mare moved off, behaving beautifully as always, heading automatically away from the home paddocks and out towards the grasslands.

Rosslyn took a deep breath of clean air. It didn't seem to calm her, instead she felt a rising urgency. The mare broke out into a brisk gallop and she let it have its head with Kylie's little face constantly before her. Kylie, full of pent-up emotions, misunderstood, breaking her heart. Walking into a deep billabong – no, she had to reject that. Kylie had a great sense of self-preservation, a fund of common sense that would get her through the worst life had to offer. At worst, she could be making herself very unhappy somewhere and possibly because of it, exposing herself to danger.

Anxiety and multiple small fears rode beside Rosslyn so that after a fruitless hour of searching, the sun seemed oppressively hot on her head and the nape of her neck. A deathly silence seemed to hang over the wild bush and she began to feel she could very nearly perish herself.

A great bird, a wedge-tailed eagle, was soaring loftily above her and she allowed herself a moment to look up at it. The sun was dazzling, a killing sun of white gold, that cast out all the shadows from under the trees. In the long, daisy-strewn grass, a wallaby stirred and bounded off before her with a great show of cocked ears and outraged independence. The heavy rain last night had filled all the water holes to overflowing and river channels were surging with muddy water. Under this blazing sky the thought of rain seemed like a miracle. Such a place of contrasts! Rosslyn felt she could have done with some raindrops now.

Kylie's favourite little tune began to run through her head. The recorded memory of Kylie's clear sweet treble, the afternoon they had been caught in the storm. On the savannahs there seemed nothing to tell that heavy rain had fallen overnight. The tall, spiky grass was bone dry, the open-faced little wild flowers shrivelling in the heat that was scorching her sensitive skin. What madness to go off without a hat! A silk scarf was no protection at all. Grass seeds were all over her slacks and her thin shirt was clinging to her back. She rode in under a brightly burning tree, smothered in scarlet brushes, ravenous for some shade.

Immediately a shrieking chorus rang out. Birds, hundreds of them! Sulphur-crested cockatoos, flapping heavily between the branches, a swish of rose pink galahs, the brilliant parrots and parakeets, too beautifully plumaged for words. They seemed to be mocking her:

You'll never find her! You're lost yourself!

She wasn't, of course. She could see the shining rim of the creek through the thick, glossy screen of trees. It was deadly, this not knowing what had happened to

Kylie. Like Ellie, she too had had some premonition of trouble from her first waking minute. Gallant little Lucy who carried her so well and so uncomplainingly deserved a drink. She would ride down to the creek, but keep to this side of it lest she lose herself in the immensity that was Belyando. If that happened, Boyd would be furious. He had given enough instructions at different times and he was a man who took obedience for granted.

The strong sun was definitely affecting her. She was panting rather quickly and feeling exhausted. Was there some sound? She listened, her ears grown acute. There *was* some noise in the undergrowth. She stared down the bank. The very thought of snakes made her feel weak, but Belyando boasted snakes in plenty. At least she didn't have to worry about crocodiles, though only that week a young pig shooter had been taken in an isolated lagoon in the Territory. This was the very edge of civilization.

Oh, where was Boyd? Her head seemed to be throbbing all of a sudden. Surely Sonia and Belinda with the jeep at their disposal would have located him by now. Ellie had called a few of the station hands up for good measure. Boyd would know what to do. *Boyd.* Six feet two of matchless energy and instant decision. Boyd was a marvel, a *man.* The odd time it paid to be a man, especially in the wilds with an imperious sun beating down on one's neck. Other times she was quite happy to be a woman.

Rosslyn set the little chestnut gently down the steep slope. It picked its way carefully, very sure-footed. The birds looked at them curiously but fell temporarily soundless. She was almost at the bottom when a goanna reared up out of the thick grass, standing erect, glaring venomously at horse and rider and lashing its forked tongue.

She nearly jumped out of her skin, let out a faint scream. The normally docile little mare shared its rider's savage shock. It reared in a panic while the goanna ran down the bank at a terrible speed, thrashing to ribbons the tender reed shoots. Rosslyn could feel herself falling, rolling, rolling, with brutally increasing momentum all the way down the slope and into the shockingly cold fast-running water. The birds shrieked the alarm for her, going frantic, circling above her marking the spot. They were no more frightened than she was. The water was raging about her, almost a torrent, carrying her downstream with the current. She let herself go with it, the breath almost knocked out of her. She was a stylish though never very strong swimmer. Style wouldn't help her now. This was no swimming pool. Even the narrow fording places, usually a trickle over stones, were running a banker, gathering volume from the headwaters.

Someone was moaning. Vaguely Rosslyn registered that it was herself. How odd! It sounded terribly ominous. There were metallic-winged wild ducks lining the banks, a shimmer of blue and green, startled spectators. Only a huge, fallen limb of a tree stopped her lightning rush. She slammed into it, breathing in painful shallow gasps. An hour ago to start out looking for Kylie, now *this*? She could die in this lovely, lonely place. Feathery arms overshadowed her. Trees. She would have to make a determined effort to help herself. If she inched along the heavy limb she might just be able to swim to the bank. On the other hand, if she dislodged the branch she and it would be swept on again. There were many deep holes and swirling accumulated debris.

The birds had fallen to looking and listening. Rosslyn would always remember them and the brown snake that hissed and slithered, then coiled itself into a tight ring. She had a sense of complete unreality as though she would soon fight out of a terrible dream, but her predicament was real enough. She would have to concentrate and move very carefully. She turned a white, despairing face towards the near bank. It would be too dreadful to die here with the water bubbling in a fury, sweeping very large rocks along like so many tiny pebbles.

From somewhere in the bush a shot rang out, then another. The air was clear. It meant they had found Kylie. Thank God! The birds took off again in uninterrupted waves of fright and abandon. They were every inconceivable colour, beating through the sky. She stared at this whirring kaleidoscope with fascination. What was wrong with her? Looking up at birds when she should have been attending to saving her own life. Her brain was making an effort, but her limbs seemed unable to obey the master signal. There was a sharp stinging pain in her temple, but only then did she become aware of it. She dared not put up a hand, but something heavier than water was trickling down her face.

A voice followed the shots. She couldn't be dreaming. A man's voice – *Boyd's*. You little fool! he would say if he ever arrived in time. Rosslyn was as weak as a kitten. She knew now it was best if she didn't try to move. She hadn't the strength to fight the swift current. Boyd, if he found her, would know instantly what to do. He would be angry. *I told you so*. She was no bushwoman, no pioneer. She knew that now definitely. He had known it all along. That brute of a goanna, the cause of it all! Lucy was quite safe, much further along the bank. Faithful Lucy, waiting patiently for a rider who couldn't get to her. Rosslyn knew she was fading a little, yet she felt quite calm, almost hopeful. Boyd would find her.

When Boyd finally broke through the heavy screen of the trees he was approaching desperation point. He couldn't remember when he had felt such fear. Not since he had been a boy and an enraged steer had come at him. Not even then. The thought of Rosslyn alone in the bush had put the fear of death into him. These were the times when his beautiful Belyando held terror. Always a woman. Women were the very devil, at the mercy of their frail strength. This was the fringe of the true rain jungle. The creeks and the numerous lagoons were overflowing. This was a major bird sanctuary and he had followed Rosslyn's tracks with the thoroughness of any two native trackers. Even so, the last ten minutes had been an agony. Then he had sighted the chestnut mare standing riderless and he had surged on again.

She should never have been allowed to go out alone.

It was altogether a disaster. Sonia, Belinda, Ellie, back at the homestead in tears – he hadn't spared a one of them. Kylie for once had been *you little wretch*! howling her head off, and serve her right! He had picked her and Melly up not a mile from the house, happily engaged in throwing boomerangs. Not that any blame could be attached to Melly, their most conscientious and reliable girl. Kylie had insisted she had been given permission and Melly had believed her. Kylie, of course, had been perfectly willing to frighten the daylights out of the entire household for an hour or so, bent on her own kind of vengeance. By the time she had thought about letting them all know her whereabouts she was too engrossed in learning how to expertly return the boomerang.

It was cruel and he had had no mercy on any of them, very much the boss man Ballinger, though his own quite frightening demeanour escaped him. He had merely been angry and affected by a shattering worry. With a girl like Rosslyn, a little city girl, anything could go wrong. Intensely preoccupied, he had driven himself for a good hour through the bush. His big black stallion was at the top of the ridge. This he had to do on foot. He bent his dark head to avoid the whipping branches, then he was out of the blanket of the trees, kicking viciously at a good four inches of snake that got in his way. The rest of it moved like greased lightning. His eyes now were on the normally crystal clear sheet of water. It was muddy, swirling and loaded with debris. Boyd's gaze whipped along its foaming course and for an instant his heart crashed right up against his rib cage and seemed to stop. It was the same feeling he had had when he was a boy and they told him his mother was dead – horror and dread, a pervading paralysis of the limbs, a blind unacceptance.

She looked scarcely more than a child, her head raised clear of the water, her bright curls firing in the slanting rays of sunlight – the only bright thing about her. The skin of her face, and her arms locked in a forked branch looked ghostly. Her head was lolled up against the black gnarled bark and there was blood matted to her hair. Boyd made the descent in record time, down along the bank and on to the water, moving with a rare sureness, a strong man, finding in a crisis additional strength. He reached for her in the yellow-ochred swirling water, striking his hand against a bouncing heavy rock, grazing the skin, sliding precariously for a moment as a stone dislodged underfoot, then he had her, prising her free, locking an arm about her, with those damn frenzied swirling birds above them, moving backwards, the best way, until he was able to stand easy and steady on his feet, with her slight, infinitely moving body in his arms.

The scratches and weals were clearly visible on the pale gold of her arms. It was a minor wound on her temple, high up, back into her hair. She looked incredibly delicate, helpless, but she was alive, and he slipped his hand over her slight breast. It was his grazed hand. It was bleeding freely, but it was wonderfully gentle. Then suddenly anger blazed up into the wild elation of relief and he began to swear violently, a man on his

177

own with a half-conscious young girl in his arms.

By the time he got back to the homestead, his mood was black so that Rosslyn, fully conscious now, her eyes enormous, found herself too much in awe of him to thank him. He obviously didn't want any thanks anyway. He stared at her hard, told her to lie back and that was that. She had seen Boyd so many ways, but his sombre, arrogant face was a shock, overwhelming. Tension showed itself in his brilliant colour-changing eyes, the uncompromising set of his mouth, the exact angle of his head. He looked very much like the portrait of his father, she decided, and *he* had been a legendary hard man.

Kylie, when she was finally allowed in to see Rosslyn, sobbed all over her dearest friend and companion. She was intensely upset. Yes, she had deliberately set out to give everyone a fright. It was extremely thoughtless and immature and she would never do it again — not on Belyando, anyway. Uncle Boyd was a bronze statue with slashing blue-green eyes. So far he had not bothered to inquire after Rosslyn's improving well-being since he had cleaned up all her cuts and given her a shot of something she didn't dare ask him. With a fainting heart she had come to recognize that she annoyed him no end.

Ellie too was thoroughly unstrung, standing at the end of Rosslyn's bed, shouting how utterly sorry she was and how dear Rosslyn had become to them all. A few minutes later Sonia and Belinda (rather forced into it) had appeared and finally Derek, for once total attention. But no Boyd. He had had enough of them all.

He had gone off in a black humour, leaving a precise set of instructions. Rosslyn was to stay in bed for the rest of the day with Ellie as watchdog and Kylie swarming all over the bed like a honey-ant, setting out her collection of puzzles and games which might pass the time.

By evening, Rosslyn decided she couldn't stand this enforced invalidism. Close to disaster she might have been, but now she was safe at the homestead in her lovely bedroom with its wonderful fourposter, a miss seemed as good as a mile. Nightmares about her ordeal she might suffer some time in the future, but for now she very much wanted to get up and perhaps listen to some of Ellie's classical recordings. A violin concerto, the Max Bruch perhaps. She adored the violin and so few people could play it with any degree of musicianship. The first time she had met Boyd (how long ago was it, an eternity, surely she had always known him?) one of the pupils had been agonizing over the simplest little piece. It could even have been a scale. She had been in a curious elated mood then. She was now. She would find Boyd and force on him her undying gratitude. He mightn't believe or want a word of it, but he would hear it all the same.

Surely he would have mellowed after a good dinner. Rosslyn had enjoyed a delicious light meal on a tray, but if anyone thought she was going to go off to sleep at eight o'clock, they were very much mistaken. She had been dozing a good part of the afternoon when Kylie had been winning hands down. Kylie had been watching her very carefully for any signs of amnesia. Kylie

179

was an odd one, a genuine character. She had in-formed the struck-speechless Rosslyn and Ellie that her father's opinion of her drawings had not troubled her unduly because she knew perfectly well they were good. Then, as in later life, Kylie would never be de-pendent on the popular vote.

Rosslyn dressed carefully in the hushed quiet of her bedroom. Kylie had been banished to bed and for once seemed keen to get there. The plain chocolate jersey with a sheen to it looked nothing on the hanger, but it clung lovingly to her young figure and it had long sleeves to cover her scratches. Actually it was stunning with her colouring, but she couldn't get the full effect of it in the mirror. It would have to do anyway, she decided.

When Belinda saw her she barely smothered a scream of dismay. 'What are you doing here? I thought you were to stay in bed.'

'No way! as Kylie says. Honestly, I couldn't stand it. Where's Boyd?'

'I should leave him alone if I were you,' Belinda cautioned. 'With any luck he just might speak to you tomorrow.'

'I can't wait until then. I want to speak to him now.'

'You never give up, do you?' Belinda smiled pleasantly, hot jealousy in her eyes. 'I'd leave well alone, dearie, if I were you.'

'But you're not me, are you?' Rosslyn said, equally pleasantly.

'With no wish to be,' Belinda snapped back. 'You

gave Boyd a bad time of it. Do you really think he wants some little schoolmarm to drown herself on his property? It would get into the papers. Besides, the merest infant would know the creeks flood after heavy rain. Soon the monsoon will set in. We'll have real rain then, rain like you've never seen it. A cyclone or two. All in all Belyando is a pretty wild place.'

'How come you want to be part of it?'

'It's Boyd I want, as you damned well know!'

Belinda like that wasn't good-looking at all. She looked rather ghastly, *and* dangerous. 'Then if he cares for you nothing can go wrong,' Rosslyn said quietly. 'Right now I only want to thank him for saving my life.'

'That's your excuse!' Belinda hissed in a fierce monotone.

'No, it's the truth. Excuse me, I *do* have a headache.'

'Then the remedy is simple. Go back to bed.'

'Cheer up, I'll be gone soon enough!' Rosslyn walked right on past Belinda, through the house and out on to the verandah. No one, least of all a woman like Belinda, could talk her out of seeing Boyd. Her skin and her hair gave off a sweet fresh fragrance, the creek water long since washed away. All her senses were attuned to the night. It was moonless, the stars blossoming brilliantly white, of a shattering radiance. She wrapped her arms around the slender, vine-wreathed white pillar and stared out over the garden. Belyando, she loved it! She might even have said it aloud. The cicadas had set up their nocturnal serenade and the air was heavy with the scent of the night-blooming lilies. She quivered and stretched up her arms slowly and luxuriously, breathing it all in. Oh, to be alive! She sighed and her face wore its dreamy captive expression.

It was obvious she hadn't seen Boyd, who was stretched out in a chair, a crystal tumbler in his hands, gently swishing the half-finished contents. When he spoke her name she almost retreated in a panic so that he stood up with one rippling motion, muffling an exclamation, and took a strong hold on her, as though she was about to fly away from him.

'What are you doing up for?' he asked with no trace of sympathy in his voice.

'I couldn't go to sleep without saying thank you.'

'For what?' he replied very moodily indeed.

'For *everything*!' she said, getting swallowed up in the nightime enchantment. 'I never seem to thank you properly.'

'That's obvious! Do me a favour, will you, little one? Don't talk. *Walk*. I seem to be under some intolerable strain.'

'You look just the same!' she said, turning up her head and staring into his face.

'Who am I supposed to be, Superman?'

'Well, aren't you?'

'Not today. Definitely not today. I'll say this for you, Rosslyn, you have terrific timing. I'll remember it to my dying day.'

'I'm sorry!' she said, hanging her head. 'I gave you a bad fright. I got a fright myself, you know. It was that damned goanna. The same one, I bet!'

'Not the same one at all!' he said briskly. 'Don't you know how many goannas there are on the property? The numbers are very likely mind-boggling. So are you, for that matter, but I'm obviously glad you're still here.'

'Thanks to you. Please let me say it.'

'Oh, I'll let you say it all right, and you can do a damn sight better than that!'

Before she had the slightest idea what he was about to do, he had bundled her up into his arms, moving off with her very purposefully to where the station wagon stood parked in the drive.

'Get in!'

It was a definite order and Rosslyn obeyed it. 'Where on earth are we going?'

'Do you want to come?' he asked with deliberate resonance.

'Yes, I do. You know I do.'

'Well then!' There was a definite hard edge in his voice that gave her fair warning. She subsided against the seat while he came around to the other side, got behind the wheel, delved for the keys. 'I guess I can drive around my own land if I want to. I dare not risk Belinda breaking in on us, and I've a strong hunch that she would. Just for spite!'

Rosslyn was feeling, very mistakenly, that he was annoyed with her and she rested her head, watching the high beam light up the track for a good five miles. When at last Boyd pulled up she let out her breath cautiously, almost frightened to turn her head and look into his eyes. A flame of excitement was there between them, a consuming, famishing fire.

'Now thank me,' he said, switching off the engine and turning to her.

'Boyd?' He seemed wondrously strange.

'*Thank me!*' he repeated, then as though fed up pulled her into his arms. She lifted her hands gently to shape his head, the crisp waves and the fine bones, but he couldn't wait for her to match his fully aroused passion. His mouth came down on hers with an insatiable desire, a fierce statement of possession. 'I never seem to have a plan with you,' he said against her soft mouth. 'It was much too late the first time I saw you.'

'Let me say thank you,' she whispered back to him so that it seemed the most exquisite endearment, her breath coming into his mouth. It awoke the deep need in him, a torrent of feeling, making him lift her across his knees, cradling her slight body as though she was infinitely precious.

'I'm not hurting you?'

'No. I wouldn't care if you were. I love you.'

'How much?' A smile silvered his voice.

'Desperately.'

'Enough to stay here with me in the wilds? It's primitive, my love, and let's face it, so am I. I want you, so badly. You're all that matters.'

'And you love me too,' she said simply.

'Yes, I do, damn you, and if I have to I'll marry you.'

'You will,' she said sweetly.

'Without a doubt. I always intended to, so don't sound so triumphant.'

She moved her face against his, warm skin, the blood pounding through her veins. Her skin like satin, his rasped silk.

'It will be lonely.'

'*Never!* Not with you.'

'Rosslyn. I think I could say your name all night. Very likely I will!' His voice had a quality of light mockery and excitement that would always touch her. Probably in the years to come when he said: 'Pass me the butter!' she would still feel the magic. She laughed at the very thought of it and tried to tell him, but he touched his mouth very lightly and deftly to the pulse in her throat, to the curve of her breast, to the delicate hollow beneath her ear. Just the trail of his fingers was almost more than she could endure without turning up her mouth to him. This was what she had been born for. She would swear to it.

'Poor Rosslyn,' he murmured, holding her. 'My poor baby! Now I'll never let you go. It's a case of what a Ballinger holds he never lets go. This afternoon I lost the last lingering desire for independence.'

'Is it bothering you?'

'No.'

Her fingers traced his beautiful, intensely male profile, touched the cleft in his chin. 'Our son will have a chin like that!' she said in a sudden premonitory flash.

She was given no time to offer more. The whole world dissolved under the touch of his mouth, the tug of his hand through her silky hair. Some journeys took a lifetime. She had been favoured. She was home, with Boyd. For always.

A GREAT IDEA!

We have chosen some of the works of Harlequin's world-famous authors and reprinted them in the 3 in 1 Omnibus. Three great romances — COMPLETE AND UNABRIDGED — by the same author — in one deluxe paperback volume.

Marjorie Norrel

Nurse Madeline Of Eden Grove (#962)
Madeline was glad to help Michael Foley realize his dream—but suddenly she knew that it wasn't her dream, and Michael was the wrong man!

Thank You, Nurse Conway (#1097)
The trouble was, Susie couldn't stop getting involved, stop caring. It wasn't just about the patients, friends, the family. Especially it was about Stephen Kendrick!

The Marriage Of Doctor Royle (#1177)
Bart Royle's proposal of marriage made Janice mad. Loving him as she did, there was no way she would enter into any marriage of convenience.

Rose Burghley

Man Of Destiny (#960)
Caroline, as governess to his nephew, was worried about meeting the Marques. But Vasco, the Marques' man of affairs, was really the difficult one.

The Sweet Surrender (#1023)
David Falcon, plagued by adoring women, picked the one girl who disliked him to keep them away. But even she had misgivings about the job.

The Bay of Moonlight (#1245)
It was such a perfect setting for romance that Sarah could hardly believe the complications and misunderstandings that bedevilled her relationship with the handsome Philip Saratola.

A GREAT VALUE!

Margaret Malcolm

The Master of Normanhurst (#1028)
Normanhurst was bound to bring heavy responsibilities. How foolish, Rilla reminded herself, to feel jealous of the very possessions Piers wanted to share with her.

The Man In Homespun (#1140)
Clive had prejudiced Caroline against Adam—but one thing was clear. Whether one liked or detested Adam, it was utterly impossible to ignore him!

Meadowsweet (#1164)
If she'd never gone to Watersmeet, never met Philippe, she would have married Keith. But once Rosamund found real love, nothing else was good enough.

Anne Durham

New Doctor At Northmoor (#1242)
Gwenny was the forgotten member of the family until she landed in hospital being treated by Doctor Mark Bayfield. The Kingslakes considered him an enemy!

Nurse Sally's Last Chance (#1281)
Sally knew she was in hot water—but young, hurt and misguided, she seemed unable to trust the one person who could have helped her.

Mann Of The Medical Wing (#1313)
She was young, elegant and attractive—but she wasn't the girl Dr. Maurice Mann had come to meet. She was a stranger, even to herself.

HARLEQUIN OMNIBUS

A Jumbo Read!!

Elizabeth Hoy

Snare The Wild Heart (#992)
Eileen had resented Derry's intrusion to make a film of the island, but she realized now that times had changed and Inishbawn must change too!

The Faithless One (#1104)
Brian had called her love an interlude of springtime madness but Molly knew that her love for him would never quite be forgotten.

Be More Than Dreams (#1286)
Anne suddenly realized her love for Garth was more important that anything else in the world—but how could she overcome the barrier between them.

Roumelia Lane

House Of The Winds (#1262)
Laurie tricked Ryan Holt into taking her on safari despite his "no women" rule—but found it was only the first round she'd won!

A Summer To Love (#1290)
"A summer to love, a winter to get over it," Mark had once joked. But Stacey knew no winter would help her get over Mark.

Sea Of Zanj (#1338)
A change of scenery, a little sun, a chance for adventure—that's what Lee hoped for. Her new job didn't work out quite that way!

Harlequin Reader Service

ORDER FORM

MAIL
COUPON
TO

Harlequin Reader Service,
M.P.O. Box 707,
Niagara Falls, New York 14302.

Canadian **SEND**
Residents **TO:**

Harlequin Reader Service,
Stratford, Ont. N5A 6W4

Harlequin Omnibus

Please check Volumes requested:

☐ Essie Summers 1	☐ Essie Summers 2	☐ Amanda Doyle
☐ Jean S. MacLeod	☐ Catherine Airlie	☐ Rose Burghley
☐ Eleanor Farnes	☐ Mary Burchell 1	☐ Elizabeth Hoy
☐ Susan Barrie	☐ Sara Seale	☐ Roumelia Lane
☐ Violet Winspear 1	☐ Violet Winspear 2	☐ Margaret Malcolm
☐ Isobel Chace	☐ Rosalind Brett	☐ Joyce Dingwell 2
☐ Joyce Dingwell 1	☐ Kathryn Blair	☐ Anne Durham
☐ Jane Arbor	☐ Iris Danbury	☐ Marjorie Norell
☐ Anne Weale	☐ Mary Burchell 2	

Please send me by return mail the books which I have checked.
I am enclosing $1.95 for each book ordered.

Number of books ordered _____ @ $1.95 each = $ _____

Postage and Handling = .25

TOTAL $ _____

Name _____

Address _____

City _____

State/Prov. _____

Zip/Postal Code _____

VW 130 260